The
Solace *of*
Monsters

Laurie **Blauner**

A NOVEL

Leapfrog Press
Fredonia, New York

Published in 2016 in the United States by
Leapfrog Press LLC
PO Box 505
Fredonia, NY 14063
www.leapfrogpress.com

Printed in the United States of America

Distributed in the United States by
Consortium Book Sales and Distribution
St. Paul, Minnesota 55114
www.cbsd.com

First Edition

ISBN: 978-1-935248-88-0

Library of Congress Cataloging-in-Publication Data

Names: Blauner, Laurie, author.
Description: First edition. | Fredonia, New York : Leapfrog Press, 2016.
Identifiers: LCCN 2016017805 | ISBN 9781935248880 (softcover)
Subjects: LCSH: Self-actualization (Psychology)--Fiction. | Identity (Psychology)--Fiction. | Self-realization--Fiction. | Psychological fiction. | BISAC: FICTION / Literary. | FICTION / Coming of Age. | FICTION / Psychological. | FICTION / Science Fiction / General. | GSAFD: Science fiction.
Classification: LCC PS3552.L3935 S65 2016 | DDC 813/.54--dc23
LC record available at https://lccn.loc.gov/2016017805

"The life of the dead is placed in the memory of the living."
—Cicero

"Fantasy, abandoned by reason, produces impossible monsters;
united with it, she is the mother of the arts
and the origin of marvels."
—Francisco de Goya

Acknowledgements

Thanks to *MAYDAY* magazine for publishing an excerpt. On page 52 the quote was from "Lolita" by Vladimir Nabokov on the second to last page of his book. The quote by William Faulkner on page 125 is from "Requiem for a Nun." The quote on page 155 is from the Bible. The poem "The Second Coming" on page 167-168 is by William Butler Yeats. All the other poetry is by Laurie Blauner.

Many, many thanks to Babs Lindsay and Rich Ives, my invaluable readers, and to Lisa Graziano and Mark Brazaitis and everyone at Leapfrog Press. Thanks also to my family and to my husband, David, with gratitude. They all made this book possible.

Contents

Acknowledgements   5

Part I – Father   9

Chapter One   11
Chapter Two   28
Chapter Three   42

Part II – The Forest   53

Chapter Four   55
Chapter Five   68
Chapter Six   80
Chapter Seven   94
Chapter Eight   106

Part III – The City   125

Chapter Nine   127
Chapter Ten   137
Chapter Eleven   151
Chapter Twelve   164

Part IV – Mara F.   175

Chapter Thirteen   177

The Author   183

Part I

Father

Chapter One

My father, Dr. F., noticed my dinner roll trembling then tumbling out of my right hand.

"I'll get you another one," he offered. "A younger one. The older ones only last so long. It could be the median or radial nerves, the digital sheath, or the flexor sublimis digitorum, or maybe the cyanoacrylate compound. Let me see it."

His usual frown ruffled his forehead like a hat. He pushed his half-eaten dinner plate, with its flurry of some bird's ribcage and legs tossed with mashed potatoes and peas, to one side. His food looked bruised. Sometimes I saw pictures of things but couldn't make all of them into a language. His shoulders drooped and his eyes grew monstrous under his thick, black eyeglasses. Light lay across the kitchen table in stitches from the bars on our windows.

"Manufacture." He stated one of the silly words to make me laugh.

I did, although it sounded horrible like teeth gnashing together.

I hesitantly unfurled my right hand and lay it on the table between us. He inspected it while I made my usual joke, "Another operation with all that anesthesia and I'll lose more of somebody else's brain cells."

To which he consistently replied, "My beautiful miracle of modern science. My lovely Mara."

He petted my hand although I knew he was careful and very

precise in his touch. He stroked my wrist scars. For a moment I envied the dead bird.

"When?" I asked, although I usually liked being imprecise.

"Now," he said. "I have something that will work."

All the air in my hollow core rushed out. The house of my body emptied out for a minute. Then I could feel my blood and organs resuming their hard work again. I thought of that bird caught flying in an unbroken sky. Now, on our plates, it was something else. My stupid heart fluttered and kicked. I wanted to draw my wings around me but they were always somebody else's wings. I wanted something that was my own, one day, an hour.

"When I turn nineteen next month I want to inhale the sky, touch a tree." I was beginning to list what I wanted to do again.

Father made a twisted face. The kitchen table seemed to knock the carcass of that bird off his plate. But it was my father jostling it accidentally with his elbow as he reached for me.

"You know, Mara, your age is simply an average of all the components. . . ." He touched my arm. He was using his soothing voice.

I could only hear ice cracking. Sometimes my senses became mixed up. If I had been a radio, then certain of my wires were crossed. I would never confess these symptoms to my father. That bird nearly leaped off of its plate and rushed toward the window. I wanted to explain to it how it would never escape.

My father was still talking, ". . . you are always more than the sum of your parts." He hugged me.

I wasn't sure. Instead I gave him a word. "Artifice."

◆ ◆ ◆ ◆ ◆

Last night I had a recurring dream that I was an ugly, moon-shape faced girl with dirty red hair in tangled strands. I was staggering down a blurry street, bumping into people, insulting them. My brain wasn't working correctly and I was fighting with everyone. I cursed someone in an alley, a man I couldn't see, and he grew angry, lifting me into the air by my neck. I saw stars, planets, planes, clouds reflected in a broken window lit by a streetlight. I saw my moony face among them and then we were swept away by black clouds into emptiness.

I didn't mind the lengthy darkness. It was the abrupt pinpoint of light that disturbed me. I screamed for my father in my sleep. Just before he ran into my bedroom, the girl's moon-face cracked into tiny little pieces and rained into my hands. It was rendered harmless and I wasn't sure I could put it back together. Underneath it, a pink brain and laddered arterial system were pulsing and beautiful.

Father ran into my bedroom without his glasses. His body crumpled in his pajamas. "Bad dreams?" He sat on my flowered coverlet.

I nodded.

"I can fix them for you."

"How do I know whether they're mine or someone else's?"

He thought for a moment. "I don't know, Mara, honey. Tell me what they were and we'll try and sort it out."

"No, I'm sure they were mine." His head tilted skeptically as though he knew I was afraid. All that cold steel, the antiseptic smells, machines rolling and whirring around me, the pain that vanished faster and faster each time.

"You know, Mara, I will always do what I can for you."

"I'm fine," I reassured him, he who took away and gave.

He patted my hand. "Complexity," he gave me before he left.

♦   ♦   ♦   ♦   ♦

I could feel my stomach digesting every bite of my dinner. Pain pinched at my head, and I heard a soft music with bright lights attached to it. My heart ran quickly ahead of me. I closed my eyes.

"You can have two hours tomorrow on the computer. Unsupervised." It was a gift, a bribe. I was rarely allowed to use the computer, relying mainly on books my father had chosen for my enrichment. The Classics he sometimes called them.

But we both knew I had nowhere to go except to the laboratory. I stood up and took my father's hand.

"My body's borrowed."

"We're all on borrowed time, honey," he told me, his precious daughter, before he unlocked the thick, heavy door to the downstairs. A variety of familiar lights tore into our skin. The machines formed a tall city around us, our own private city. I lay down on the padded table. He strapped me down. He caught me staring at the Photographs, the Mother and Daughter contentedly surrounded by trees and pet animals, the Scientist standing in front of a building at his school. The Scientist gave my father his first interesting word, "Complicity." I glanced at the Photographs before every operation to say hello.

We each had collected scars.

My father's forehead had a circle of light attached to it. His wild white hair escaped from the top of his head, a blue paper mask covered his face. His glasses peeked out from above the blue edge. He wore his beige gloves and the table with instruments sat near his waist. He held my plastic mask aloft as I writhed beneath the straps.

His eyes followed mine to see where I was looking. "Look past the person."

I didn't always understand his lessons. But it wasn't him getting the operations, stuck in bed for months, unable to move some arm or leg or worse, not capable of eating, sleeping, hearing, or seeing. I pushed his arm and my mask away with my available fingertips, and then I held on to it. No piece of me went unnoticed.

"You're the future, darling Mara. You're my whole life," he reminded me.

I tingled inside. I stuck out my makeshift tongue at him. I released his arm. "Don't be abstract," I chided him. I wanted specifics. How was I the future?

He didn't answer me. The mask he lowered onto my face

smelled how I imagined lake water stank, dank, wet, and earthy. Cones of light crossed my eyes and those trees and animals from the Photographs grew closer, started breathing with me. Deep breaths. Deeper. I began collapsing back into myself. I remembered hiding from my father, behind some jars of pickled hooves and snouts, human livers, bladders, brains, hearts, ears, and intestines in the lab a long time ago. Skulls lined one shelf. He ignored my racing and crouching and giggling. I had asked him where he got all the parts in the jars.

"Sweetheart, you don't want to know." He patted my hand. "That's for me to worry about."

Where else could I go?

"I'm the future seen through a glass of cold water," I murmured. That dead chicken was pecking at my side as a beautiful blue color surrounded me.

"Where did that come from?" He was talking to himself already, a knife in his hand, his extra surgical eyepiece dangling over his enlarged eyes, the steady circle of light from his forehead. Everything in the laboratory was ready, humming. "We create ourselves," he whispered to me from very far away.

◆　◆　◆　◆　◆

I searched for blood as I awoke slowly in the empty room. I thought I could taste the blood, rich and metallic in my mouth, but there wasn't any pooled there. I could smell it oozing from my right hand, syrupy and like iron, as though I was another one of my father's machines that needed to be oiled. When I lifted my head, I didn't see any visible bleeding, only a new hand with stitches and something clear and dripping. I tried to squeeze it but it was stiff and I was still strapped to the table.

When I was a Childcloud and newly born Dr. F. told me, "Sometimes one small pain seems bigger than the whole." I tried not to concentrate on the incisions. I tried to find my way out of my body. I could hear my father's voice in the office next to the lab.

"I don't understand her imagination." He was talking into his tape machine. I could hear the clicking and sputter of it. "Where does it come from?"

He was saying that I was different.

"And we're only beginning to scratch the surface." Click. Footsteps came toward me.

At the end of this operation I imagined a white bird that fought its way up and out of my throat. It flew away, leaving me sick and empty.

Father's face looked wan and bloodless as he released the straps. He peered at my new hand. "It looks good, sweetheart. I tried my new adhesive compound, which might further enhance your muscle strength. I also added a mole to your right cheek." He was attaching a bandage to the side of my face.

My eyes flew to the Photographs and there it was, the dark speck on the Daughter's cheek that I hadn't noticed before. My heart stuttered but I should have known.

I opened my mouth. Only a groan escaped. Sometimes, after more than one operation in one day, my voice became an unintelligible growl from so much anesthesia. I believed that I was the sum of all the people Father had used. Father said that everyone had parts of all the people they had known inside of them. I mismanaged my small happinesses, a day without aches, noise I could almost hear from a street that was described in a book, or the morning sky ablaze through the bars on our windows, making striped patterns on the walls. And no piece of me went unnoticed with my father. He was vigilant.

I had wanted to whisper to him that the damaged parts of me loved the damaged parts of him.

"Mingle," I croaked as I sat up. My father turned around, he was busy cleaning instruments, wiping the machines, slowly turning everything off. His reflection expanded and contracted on the stainless steel. He was behind the table with the large microscope.

"Thank you for the word."

"No. I WANT to mingle." I finally got it out of my throat.

"With whom or to do what? You can order anything you want over the computer. Would you like a new dress or shoes? It's the same as being there."

"No, it's not. I want the world. I want to touch it." I pushed a finger toward his back but it didn't reach him. I was exhausted.

"You're nearly perfect," his back said.

"No one is perfect," I sighed, hoping my new fingers would work well. I carefully slid off the table a little bit of me at a time. My legs were stiff and feathery. Father pulled his gloves off and helped me. "Next time I want a tail."

"Very humorous, Mara."

"I want to actually be out there. Meet people. See places. So many different worlds are described in books. Is there a different world for everyone?" He wasn't answering me. What was he frightened of?

Father perched his glasses down further on his nose. "I'm afraid of what the world will do to you." He looked sad again.

I smiled a crooked anesthesia smile. "What about what I could do to the world?"

◆　◆　◆　◆　◆

Soon after I was a Childcloud and newly born Father began bringing home flowers, daffodils whose yellow petals, filled with sunlight, illuminated our ceiling and walls and turned them yellow, white roses with their perfume and heavy, layered heads, and red tulips whose repetition I saw around the outside of our house from my window which disturbed me. He taught me their names, smells, and their particular needs (water, soil, sunlight). They usually ended up on our floor, scattered, crushed, abandoned behind furniture, or mummified and forgotten in vases. I was reluctant to touch them. The earliest ones had become green pulp between my fingers.

"You don't know your own strength, darling daughter." His eyebrows crossed in a worried way. "Agility," he gave me.

Then he began bringing home mice from his research job, the extras. One at a time. I didn't do any better with the mice at first. They turned inside out in my fists, all fur, bones, blood, and organs until I learned patience and how to slow down time to my advantage. I let the mice gnaw my fingers, felt their tiny clawed feet on my skin, along my sleeves, and at the back of my neck. They tickled me with their tails and feet and fur, making me laugh, a large sound which flung one of the mice onto the floor. Then I accidentally crushed it.

"Unintentional," I told my father.

"We'll keep trying."

One day he brought home two mice together, unlocking the heavy front door, holding them aloft in one cage. Then he locked the door behind him. Father was the only one with keys to all our locks. He was careful. I could sniff the outdoors for a moment when he slipped in and out of that door. I thought of large pale shapes passing our house, a tinkling like coins falling from a pocket, people grinning and pointing at me. Maybe it had been a memory.

"Let's go down to the lab," he said.

"Overwhelmed," I explained to him when he placed both mice in my palm inside the laboratory. I didn't hurt them although my hand involuntarily began opening and closing like a wing. I tried to pet one with the outstretched finger of my other hand. It bit me, which surprised me. One mouse leaped to the floor and the other jumped into the nest of my dark uncombed hair. While trying to remove the mouse from my hair I burst its skin, its blood and organs became a wet, red pulp as it plopped to the floor.

"Maybe we need to practice," my father replied.

I stood there crying, my arms hanging at my sides. The other tiny mouse had disappeared in our house. "How do I know I'm real?" I blubbered.

"You killed something, didn't you?" Father was bent down, cleaning. "We kill the things we care for. And it's always a mistake."

I cried harder.

I lay on the operating table. "Fix me."

"I can't," he said, looking forlorn.

"I read on the computer that cerebral cortex neurons replace themselves every seven to ten years, as do most of the other cells in our bodies. We become totally new people every decade or so." This was a story I liked to tell myself. It made me hopeful. I moved my wet face towards his. "It's immoral to kill any living creature, even if you don't mean to."

He patted my shoulder. "I know, Mara." His eyes grew wet too.

◆　◆　◆　◆　◆

I had been trying to understand the complexities of the mirror in my bathroom since I was a Childcloud. Was that me in there? Did I do everything my image did? I searched for anomalies in my skin and other features but the mirror was disturbing. I stopped gazing at it for a while. I was pleasantly surprised some time later when I looked again.

I had been a shattered woman who was patched together again. I cut my dark shaggy hair into both long and short strands that reached to my chin. Brown clumps were trying to grow from my scalp in small bursts. Later I noticed my short nose, brown eyes sunken into my face. Sometimes a round, pale moon face wanted to emerge from my own thin oval one. I had long eyelashes and my eyebrows seemed unfinished. The first time I peered at myself I had been passing the mirror. I crawled back to determine what was there. I watched myself breathe. I watched myself turn around and scratch my cheek.

"Reflection," I whispered to myself, understanding.

I had raised red scars then. Some turned white and itched but they didn't hurt anymore. I was the fifth Mara, developed from the failures of the others before me. I opened my mouth and inspected it the same way my father had. I understood that I was his greatest and worst creation. But then I was also my own. The scars faded rapidly and were replaced by thin lines that resembled wrinkles. Then the wrinkles faded. I was stitched together and didn't see another like me in my limited books or computer time.

I had tried moving more delicately, practicing lifting small objects with grace in front of the mirror. My joints were angular and full of errors. My arms and legs seemed awkward. I discovered that everything that came out of the body had a purpose. And the beginnings of actions arrived from my thoughts. I tried to listen.

Inside my skin did the other Maras wait and stir? Could I separate into distinct selves? Once I had seen and understood the mirror and the Photographs, I knew what Dr. F. had made me for. But was my purpose the same as his?

I was breakable.

♦　♦　♦　♦　♦

After the mice Father brought home a mangy gray cat. Father locked me into my living quarters, my bedroom and bathroom, every day when he went out to work or shop and then again at night. My bookshelf with my ninety seven books, were all chosen by Father for a reason. "Classics whose titles I recognize so they must describe the complexities of life," he theorized. I had read several of them at least twice, *To Kill a Mockingbird*, *The Metamorphosis*, *Lolita*, and *The Adventures of Huckleberry Finn*. But because Father hadn't read them we couldn't discuss them. He kept the computer in his room. I couldn't wander around his bedroom or the rest of the house. He left me food in a small refrigerator. He was afraid. I feared the dying gray cat whose fur looked pasted with sweat. Father tossed her out of a cardboard box into our living room. There was a screech inside of her, then she gingerly sniffed my ankles and calves. She rubbed her whiskers on my knees after I sat down.

I didn't understand what she wanted or what her purpose was. I tried not to seize her and rub her fur under my nose. I tried to ignore her, hoping she'd tell me where she'd been, what she'd accomplished, what the world was like. What had she done to end up in our house?

"She likes you," Father guffawed. "Now you have to name her."

"We'll see if she lives."

"It doesn't really matter," he said. But I wasn't sure whether he meant it or not.

"I'll call her Gloves. She pushes into her body in a certain way." I didn't want to disturb or frighten her. "Gloves, what's it like to have a tail?" I inhaled her delightful animal odor.

Father swiveled around, smiled. "If you really, really want one, I can give you a tail for a day."

"No thanks." I was uncertain whether he was joking or not. Poor Gloves. What else could she lose living here?

I shut Gloves out of my room, fearful of flinging her in my sleep or accidentally stepping on her when I was barely awake. We were locked apart most of the day anyway and I wondered what she did. Sometimes I heard her scratching or meowing. I brooded over her and what it was like to be unhuman. I found her sleeping on a rug yesterday while Father was making dinner. I carefully neared her, tiptoeing, then scooting on my hands and knees. When her yellow eyes flew open, my brown ones were focused on hers. She didn't scream or run away. She closed her eyes again, dropped her head onto her paws and fell back asleep. I liked her and had much to learn. I was glad she was with us. I was determined not to ruin her.

"She's a test you know. That's all," Father said cruelly.

"Irreparable."

"You couldn't think of a more intelligent name for her after reading all those books I've brought you?" His keys jangled in his hands. I could see the ghost of myself reflected in the lens of his eyeglasses.

"I'll work on it." My mind was churning. "I could call her God."

Father smirked. "Don't be ridiculous, Mara. There's no such thing as God."

"Couldn't you create God?"

Father didn't answer. He went downstairs to the laboratory saying, "Don't forget your hand exercises."

But my new hand had adapted to my body already. I didn't need the exercises. My cell regeneration was accelerating. I didn't know why. It could have been Father's new adhesive. I wasn't going to tell my father.

I followed Gloves around our house for a few hours to gain some insight into her mind. I would make sure I didn't harm her. She rubbed against furniture, made a low murmuring sound that wasn't unpleasant, smelled the cushions of our sofa, stalked a button and rolled around the floor with it. Her ears twitched at any little sound. I discovered that I could hear the noises she could if I concentrated hard enough. She seemed content until she suddenly swerved and dashed at shadows. I stayed out of her way, observing her the same way my father had first watched me, as though he was uncertain what could happen, a form of curiosity and anxiety.

I had been contemplating how haphazard her running about appeared as I sat on the maroon sofa. I must have fallen asleep because when I woke up, Gloves was curled up on my knees. I was terrified and wanted to scream. Instead I tried to gently push her off with the back of my hand. She didn't budge. She shifted and became a tighter ball of gray fur. Was she sick? Unhappy? Distracted? Accelerating or falling apart? I knew nothing about her, only that Father had decided she wasn't a good test subject for an experiment at his job. My mouth tasted like dust and a purple light hurled itself around my head. My fingertips grew numb from pressing them deeply into the cushions. My teeth and jaws clenched and unclenched. Muscles I'd forgotten along my arms and shoulders rose and grew tense. I began to settle down. I tried to relax the knotted, noticeable deltoids, the trapezius, and the levator anguli scapulae. I was unable to reach a calming pill Father left for me in the kitchen. I hadn't destroyed her yet, and she looked comfortable. I touched her back lightly, feeling each tiny vertebra.

"You are going through a period of diapause," I told the animal, understanding her need for rest.

A memory arrived of rain dripping from enormous primitive leaves in a thick tangled forest. The odor of wetness and sour breath permeated everything. It was hot and humid. A black man was yelling at me, and I held a metal stick in my hands. A car with large tires was nearby, waiting. I glimpsed yellow eyes curtained by all those leaves. The eyes were suddenly running toward me. A creature with spots and bigger than Gloves was almost on top of me, her claws extended, her icicle teeth visible.

I had managed not to move. I wanted to return the memories that weren't mine but I learned from them. I stared at Gloves' needle-thin claws. I tried to very gently pry her mouth open with my little finger but she'd have none of that. I determined that I could hurt her more than she could hurt me. So I waited another two hours or so until she decided to leave my legs and go eat some food Father had left out for her. I was stiff and unbending when I stood. But by then I'd grown very fond of her.

◆　◆　◆　◆　◆

The next morning I watched Gloves hiding pieces of paper, the twist tops from bread, as well as bottle lids, and pens. Then she would rediscover them. They were like someone else's memories. I wanted to join in, throw crumpled paper balls or conceal test objects like bookmarks, old equipment knobs or cogs or shoe laces to see if she could find them. But I didn't want to become Father or become distracted and forgetful of Gloves' whereabouts or actions.

"Amicable," I gave my father.

"Psychological disaster," he gave me back. We both laughed. There were layers of understanding and misunderstanding between us. He, of course, was a part of the world and I wasn't. I could never be sure what he was thinking or how much more he knew.

Father laid out my lessening medicines and pills every morning on the yellow kitchen table at breakfast before he left for work. I had asked him, "Is it because I'm getting better?"

"Mara, you get better and better each day. Maybe it's because of my latest concoction." He smiled with his dazzling white teeth.

I thought about asking him about his beautiful teeth but I already knew his answer. "If you want some new teeth I'll get you some."

He always left me my special pill to soothe me in case I became upset while he wasn't home. I usually tucked it into my pocket before I was locked in my bedroom upstairs. But Gloves leaped up on our kitchen table and began playing with my special pill Father had just placed there. Before I could stop her she sniffed it, tentatively licked it, then swallowed it and ran into another room. We chased her as she darted under chairs and tables from room to room.

"I'm going to be late for work," Father lamented.

"But this is Gloves," I argued.

When father and I found her in his bedroom, she was walking in circles in front of his bed and then she fell to the floor on her side. I was very alarmed. I descended onto my hands and knees and entreated Father to fix the motionless Gloves. I begged and begged. "I have these holes in my face and they're all crying in your direction," I told him. "Please," I was whimpering.

"I'll have to call in sick," he stated with a thread of annoyance in his voice.

Father looked at me askew a moment and then whisked Gloves into his arms and disappeared downstairs into the laboratory for a long time, locking the door behind him. I sat and waited outside the door. I think two nights passed. I couldn't tell because so much darkness surrounded me and I didn't move to eat or sleep as it didn't seem necessary and I might miss Father emerging with Gloves.

When he finally came back upstairs I crawled up to him with my stiff legs, wrapped my arms around his knees and looked up at him.

He nodded at me. "Give me a few more days."

♦   ♦   ♦   ♦   ♦

One night I awoke to animal howling. I had been dreaming about anatomical sketches. First the bones, then organs, arterial system, muscles, lastly skin. The creatures were layered, one necessary part of them following another, until they were complete. They resembled a man, a woman, then a dog, a cat, a rat. They became all mixed up, becoming mythical beings with human and animal sections. Beasts I had never discovered before in books. Had I actually seen them? Maybe one of the Maras had. Or they had been someone else's dream. The howling stopped after a short time. I felt Gloves' absence keenly. I still looked for her everywhere she had been, but she was never there.

As I was sitting up in my bed, the mouse that had escaped before hurled itself across my bed and ran into a corner and disappeared. I turned on a light and sniffed at the wall to find it, but I couldn't figure out where it had gone.

Finally one morning Father carried the cat upstairs and placed her, standing, on our floor. But she appeared shattered. Her gray fur was more matted and whitening on the tips. She had scars crisscrossing her body. A bulge protruded from her stomach. One eye looked lower than the other one. When I tried to touch her back, she snapped at me.

"This isn't Gloves," I told Father.

He scoffed. "You're too involved in details. You've lost sight of the bigger picture."

I tried following her around the house as usual. But she never played or rested on my legs or explored anything except the front door, which she scratched at incessantly. We ignored each other and I grew lonesome watching her. Some days I couldn't look at her at all. I retreated to my room; shut the door as Father required. I lay on my bed.

Father had commented, "One of you might have grown allergic to the other during her recovery."

I missed her old self. Gloves One.

"A souvenir," I told Father. "A memory." I had pains in my body that were new when I thought about her and medicine didn't help me.

One night Father came home carrying a pizza for dinner and Gloves ran between his legs while the door was open. She was very fast. Father gasped, handed me the hot pizza. I smelled the outside, felt the food warm against my hands. He hurried outside, where I wasn't allowed, shut the door behind him, searched for her for a few minutes but he returned empty-handed.

"She's long gone," he explained, shaking his head.

◆　◆　◆　◆　◆

The Story of Touching God

I lived with strangers. People and creatures came in and out of my house at night. I didn't know any of them. Sometimes in the evening, when I was lonely I closed my eyes, listened to their unfamiliar noise. Their proximity calmed me. I wasn't alone anymore. I didn't know why they visited. I had locked them out before but they always found a way inside. I didn't interact with them. Sometimes I tried to recognize them in daylight.

At night they whispered about me. "Did you see what she just did?"
"She's so strange."

I would open my eyelids; see blue, brown, yellow, or green eyes
watching me. I studied them. I listened. I wanted to know them. They
studied me. They listened. I didn't know what they wanted. One day
a gray cat visited and stayed. I found her splayed on my living room
rug. I didn't know what to do with her. I had never taken care of
anything before. She needed food and water and she ignored the dan-
gers of my body. She brushed my legs, rubbed my elbows, nibbled food
from my ignorant fingers. We circled one another, smelling, nudging.
I called her God. One day she allowed me to smooth her bristling fur
and pry a claw. I was ecstatic until she broke into little, gray pieces, a
puzzle I couldn't fit together again.

The strangers returned that night and swept God's pieces up with
a broom into a small, gray pile. They put her in a bag. As they were
turning to leave they whispered to one another, "I told you she couldn't
be trusted."

"But I cared for her more than myself," I yelled.

"That's not enough," they answered. They shook the bag of God
onto the floor in front of the door to my house. I wanted to cry. They
shaped what was left of her into a cat. God suddenly stood, all in one
piece, and walked out with the strangers on her wobbly legs.

I hid my first story deep inside one of my books so Father couldn't
find it.

Chapter Two

While I was thinking about Gloves I heard Father's car, an old white Ford, arrive. Father presented me with black heeled shoes and a blue silk dress that shimmered with available light and flowed softly over everything. I tried it on immediately in the bathroom near the kitchen. I flung my blue jeans and old plaid shirt on the floor. In the mirror the dress shrugged along my elbows, thighs, scars, and bumps. It felt lovely against my skin.

"All these beginnings are deceptive," I told him when I emerged.

"Those books seem to be helping you. Your vocabulary is improving immensely. Do you need more books?"

I shook my head, turned around and around in the kitchen, feeling the watery dress splashing around me. "Are we going somewhere?"

Father studied me expectantly. One eyebrow raised itself. "Where do you want to go, Mara?"

"Anywhere, as long as I can wear this dress." I was twirling in circles, the hem of the dress blew wide, floated in the air.

"You know the world is a very difficult place." He began his usual explanation. "So many disasters happen: wars, famine, shootings, rapes, killings, bombs. People lie, Mara. They tell you one thing when they really mean another. It's complicated. They steal. They laugh at you and hurt you in ways you can't even imagine." Sometimes he outlined details from "current events," a child set on fire, a mother buried alive, a city nearby whose young protestors were shot.

"Nearby?" I had asked.

"No," he shook his head, "not close at all." He must have heard the excitement in my voice.

But I could remember some things and imagine some others. Father already admitted that. "What about the good events in the world? I have read stories about people's generosity, caring, and hope, people trying to understand other people, people trying to help one another." There were all those experiences waiting to be experienced. What about the lovely dress?

"Kindness is rare. Believe me, Mara, I know."

I didn't always understand my father, yet he was overflowing with his own knowledge. I searched his eyes, hidden by his glasses, and he was far away, as though he was sorting through his own memories, arranging the most horrible ones in front. They were proof enough for him.

"Thank you for the drunken dress." I wanted to make him happier.

He finally laughed. "Rambunctious."

It sounded nice to me, his tinkling giggle and my grating roar. "Am I animal, vegetable, or mineral?"

He stopped laughing. "Some of the earlier prototypes had some unusual parts but you're very human, Mara. Why do you ask? What do you think you are?"

I wanted to hold the Photograph in front of me. "I don't know."

"You're my daughter."

I didn't want to ask about the other one, or the four before me. They were inside of me. And all of us wanted to escape. I didn't know how to do it. My two unsupervised hours on the computer had already been used up and I wasn't allowed on the computer often. I had sent a group message that said, "Help! I'm being held captive in a laboratory where I'm being experimented on." Online I was thevillagersarerestless. And I was a forty-year-old overweight housewife who collected porcelain dolls whose eyes flipped open and called me "Mama." I had no idea where we lived.

The only reply I received was from monkeyman who answered, "Ha, ha. Aren't we all?"

I asked, "Are you made of monkey parts?"

"What do you think?"

I concluded that I was better off searching for more factual material, like what types of trees, bushes, and flowers grew in different states, and medical information. No one knew what to believe in cyberspace. Or I could view blue shoes to match my new dress.

Father had a pensive look on his face, his white hair sprayed out from his head, his glasses slipped down his nose. "Let's have a guest over for dinner tomorrow night. I'll cook. You can wear that dress."

"A guest! Here!" I screamed. I imagined that mouse scurrying back to its hole, that dead chicken spreading its wings to fly, Gloves missing us and hurrying back home. Somebody else's heart was churning. "We've never had a guest before. A human guest?"

"Yes, Mara," Father chuckled. "A human male."

"Who?" I screamed at him, not meaning to be so loud.

"I'm not sure yet. It'll be a surprise."

"Why?" I blurted out, thinking of the experiments with mice.

"It's time to be around another person. You're ready. You can see a bit of the world that way." Father chuckled.

This was probably another one of Father's tests.

Father turned away from me and whispered into his cell phone, which he hardly used at home, and was constantly attached to his body. He swerved toward me. "We have a day to get prepared. I'll teach you etiquette."

"Etiquette." I laughed at the word.

"You know. Things like not to lick your plate or gnash your teeth at someone."

But when he demonstrated how to contain myself and my movements, I remembered being around other people. I understood the utensils and unnecessary, polite conversations. An image returned to me, one of children fleeing from my outspread female hands. The fingers had long, red fingernails, unlike my current hands. The image felt as though it was stolen more from my future than my past. The children's faces were lit with fear.

I was sitting near the kitchen window as darkness began creeping through the window bars and across the yellow table, turning it blue. "Who invented cats?"

"No one, Mara, they simply evolved over time."

I wondered if I could evolve into a cat over time. "Can I die?"

"Yes, you certainly can." Father's face crimped in anguish and all his wrinkles were visible. His eyes, behind his glasses, began to tear.

I thought of Gloves. Was she dead or alive? There was so much I wanted to learn. I juggled my silverware with fast motions so the knife, fork, and spoon were misplaced in a little pile. I gazed at Father's surprised expression. Then I hurried them back to their rightful places. I had bent the fork by mistake.

"When did you get so dexterous? Let me see your hands. You have to be very careful with your increasing strength." He unfurled his own hands.

"Yes." I glanced pitifully at the bump in the fork.

◆　◆　◆　◆　◆

That night my body was tangled in my sheets and sweat poured in rivulets along my old scar lines. The bars on our windows reminded me of fences. I pushed back the curtains to see the moon and some stars scattered above the trees. I wasn't supposed to look outside.

"These curtains are for YOUR protection," Father reiterated, "although we're isolated here and there's no one nearby for at least five miles." Every so often I was aware of the noise of a car or bus or truck passing by, its headlights scraping the sides of our house with light. But it was on a distant road.

I rose, wandered around my bed, listening for a narration

from a pine tree or an animal rustling outside. Maybe the lost mouse would whisper some valuable information into my prone ear. No creature was voiceless. I just needed to learn their language. In the pure dark I didn't know where my body ended and night began. That was a relief. But I could see well enough in the moonlight. Was a neighbor coming for dinner or one of Father's friends from his research job? He didn't like talking about work unless he wanted to complain.

"They treat me like I'm nothing, Mara. All because of some assumptions I made on a project after the accident." Father refused to talk about the accident. "It was my fault. It was all my fault." His head tried to bury itself in his hands.

Father told me to follow his lead with the guest and not talk much or ask any questions.

Before I finally fell asleep, I inventoried my newest parts: my most recent hand, new kidney, ear, left foot, the useless mole, several vertebrae, a kneecap. My face had remained stable for a long time. Everything felt good, in working order.

An enormous black beetle was floating facedown in the center of the East River in New York City. Tall buildings surrounded the water and people gathered along the sides to watch the insect wash by. Hardly any trees adorned the banks and once a gull tried to alight on the hard back of the beetle. After a second it flew off. Some of the beetle's black stick-legs churned in the river. I couldn't tell if it was trying to swim or to keep from drowning. I'd seen a photograph of the East River once in a book. Children, families, bicyclers, pets all lined up along the beetle's route. Finally the giant beetle reached the end of the river and was stopped by a large chunk of cement. People crowded near the insect's desperately pedaling legs. They began throwing anything they had at the flailing beetle: keys, books, hats, eyeglasses, briefcases, shopping bags. One young boy tried to hurl his bicycle. It missed hitting the insect but formed a wave that turned the beetle onto its back, where its legs pumped in the air. When I looked closely, the beetle's face was my own.

I woke up startled, with my head hurting.

Was I hard-shelled and difficult? What have you done, Father? I found something solid and round rolling around under my covers, at the bottom of my bed, like a pea. When I threw back the sheets I discovered that I had lost the top joint of the big toe of my new left foot. Some blood had dried and flaked off my skin. I hadn't noticed any pain and hadn't woken up with any in the night. I brushed the brittle dark scabs onto the floor. I picked up the withered top toe joint and threw it into my toilet, flushed it down. The rest of my toe was fine without it. My body was growing mutinous.

I wouldn't tell my father. It seemed a bad omen.

♦ ♦ ♦ ♦ ♦

The guest's name was Gregory, Greg for short. I vomited before he arrived, which I hadn't done since Father once had a problem with the anesthesia and one time after a stomach operation when I was a Childcloud. Our rooms slanted when I stood upright in my bathroom. I saw fireworks when I glanced in the mirror and wiped my mouth. I thought I noticed the loose mouse scuttling over my bathroom tile and hurrying into the hallway in my peripheral vision. When I peered closely, nothing was there.

"Don't get too excited about Gregory, Mara. He's dumb as a post." Father's eyebrows ran around his forehead as he wiped my mouth. "I shouldn't have told you about his coming ahead of time."

"It's an occasion to wear this dress." I twirled and the blue silk tried to go someplace else. I wore my new black shoes, and Father hadn't noticed my missing toe yet.

I believed I heard Gloves howling outside our house just before Gregory tried ringing our defunct doorbell repeatedly. When Father opened the door for Gregory a soft, brown moth flew inside. I wanted to hunt that moth down and breathe it inside of me.

Then I could have part of the world outside beneath my skin and it would remain a part of me forever. I could briefly smell grass and dandelions and warm sunlight, which I took to be summertime since we didn't need any heat in the house.

I had learned from Gloves that I could sniff people and see where they'd been. I restrained myself from doing that to Gregory, who waited at the door behind Father.

Once, when I was a Childcloud I told Father, "I smell smoke and something bitter and liquid. And you urinated recently."

"Cigarettes and one whiskey. And yes, I did. It's the anniversary of the accident. But I won't do that again. Besides Mara, it's impolite to smell people."

So I tried not to. But I did fabricate stories about where Father had been and what he'd been doing from any odors I could detect from far enough away. I'd tell the stories only to myself.

At some distance Gregory smelled of soil and cut grass and some old greasy food, shampoo, deodorant, something antiseptic, apples, and he, too, had urinated recently. He had dark wavy hair that had a brisk, sweet odor and flapped over his forehead. He had brown eyes and pleasant features. He was shorter than both my father and I. His hands seemed uprooted and everywhere, carving descriptions in the air when he talked. He was much younger than Father. I closed my eyes for a moment and listened to his robust pulmonary system and his strong, steady breathing. He was healthier than Father, but not as vigorous as me. Even with all the operations to repair me, I knew I might crush Gregory unintentionally. That was why Father and I rarely touched one another fondly. And why I had to touch anyone or anything so delicately.

Gregory was just inside our door, and he was saying, "There's quite a forest around this house . . . and I didn't even know you had a daughter." He smiled at me and his face lit up in a good way, as though he was happy that I had come into existence. His hair slapped at the sides of his head. Father quickly locked the front door behind him.

"Welcome," Father said in a false manner I'd never seen before.

Father sat us in the dining room at the large table usually reserved for books or papers or the scant mail that arrived for Father. I'd spied on the mailman a few times, but he walked briskly to and from our house, and I knew Father wouldn't like me brushing the upstairs curtains aside since someone might see me. Father opened the revolving door to the kitchen and a host of odors emerged: chicken, rice, and broccoli.

He left Gregory and me alone at the table, and I grew nervous when he spoke. My lungs and mouth became dry and stale as something else inside ripened.

"Someone at work mentioned a car accident. I thought all his family had died. But I see that isn't true. What's your name?"

"Mara." It was my first time almost lying because I hadn't corrected him and explained. I noticed our flowered wallpaper tearing itself away from our walls above his head and the mouse's head darted out from a hole and then it popped back inside. It was distracting.

He stood and shook my new hand across the table. "Gregory. I see you have a few scars but not many. When was it? Seven or eight years ago?"

Father quickly returned. He said, "What have you two been talking about? Job rumors? Or what's for dinner?"

We both shook our heads.

Father placed our steaming dinner plates in the middle of the table so we could take what we wanted. "Be careful what you say in front of Mara, Greg. She's very intelligent and has a quick and unusual mind." Gregory piled food onto his plate and began eating.

I smiled at the chicken, proud of any thoughts that were uniquely mine.

Gregory said, "At work they sure are finding us the worst and most boring jobs to do, sterilization, cleaning. At least we get to use the microscopes every once in a while. Right, Doctor? Hey, what did you do to get demoted? I played a practical joke on somebody and ended up in that lousy facility."

"Mara," Father said to me, "Gregory is my boss." Father gnawed at a piece of chicken and spit the bones out. He turned to Gregory and said, "You must have heard something about me."

Gregory's face and ears reddened. He mumbled, "I heard you doctored some research results at the school and it was a doozy."

"Ah, the important part is WHICH research results, the recombinant or the chimeric DNA?" Father was still eating.

"Inconsequential," I gave them. Father and I laughed. Gregory looked perplexed.

"I heard it was some kind of vaccine for a chimpanzee cloning program and that because of it, all the experimental clones died. I heard they had to shut the whole thing down."

Father banged his fist on the table. "Clones! All people want is cheaper meat to eat. Cloning couldn't replicate people. The clones were genetically identical to the originals but different. Like fraternal twins. They didn't even look the same."

"Are you saying you tried it out on people?" Gregory's jaw dropped open.

Father commenced eating as though Gregory hadn't said anything. "The body—no actually for me it is my mind—always insists on something. Something it needs." He looked back and forth between Gregory and me. That was enough explanation for Father. "How about some wine?" Father asked us both.

"What's wine?" I asked.

"Fermented grape juice." Father looked at me askance. "I'm surprised you haven't read about it in one of your books."

I wrinkled my nose. "It sounds disgusting. What's grape juice like?"

"She was home schooled and she doesn't get out much, Greg." Father went downstairs, leaving Greg and me alone again.

I didn't know there was anything downstairs, in the laboratory and office, that wasn't mechanical, surgical, or a body part.

"So, Mara, what do you do all day?" Greg was reaching for more food.

"I read a lot. I play sometimes." He must not have noticed the bars on the windows since all the curtains were closed.

"I'm more interested in the play part." He grinned. I wasn't sure why.

"I can make my fingers into puppets."

"I'd like to see that sometime." He sounded disappointed.

"Tell me about your work with my father."

"I'm sure it's really boring for your father after everything's he's done. It's mostly grunt work. I bet the Doctor could do better work than the scientists we clean up after."

"What kind of research are they doing there?"

"They don't even bother to tell us and we don't have clearance anyway." His head hung to his chest. "But your father thinks it's some kind of stem cell research. He's figured this out from their garbage, from their fucking garbage." He seemed excited about that.

I was finding the guest's human nature different than what I had been taught, gestures belying what was said, a vulnerability, an admiration for my father, which I shared. Things were more complex than I had imagined.

Father returned with an old suitcase that had travel tags still attached to the handles. I had never seen it before. He lifted out two bottles of wine in his fists.

"Now you're talking, Doctor."

He poured wine into a glass, lifted it up, swirled the wine around. "You have to let it breathe first, Mara."

I made my grinding laugh and Greg stared at me. "It doesn't have any lungs. The grapes can't come back to life."

Father ignored me. He sniffed at the wine and drank some. "It's just an expression. You inhale to gather the aroma and enhance the taste."

"I thought that would be impolite."

37

"Then you can drink it," Father continued, ignoring me and drinking more wine. "Here," and he poured a glass for Greg and one for me. He looked at me.

I'd read about wine-making but I knew almost nothing about wine itself. I imitated my father although I didn't see the wine breathing at all. It smelled of fruit and springtime and rotten leaves, vinegar, and something bitter and sweet all at once. I tasted it and I could feel it plodding down my throat and making a warm rush for my gurgling stomach. The strange, sharp moisture of the wine filled the rest of me. Father and Greg could drink the wine faster than I could.

"Here's to working at that shit hole." Greg lifted his glass to the overhead light so it shone various shades of a deep red. Then he emptied it in one gulp down his throat. His hair flew in his face as though it was having a discussion with him.

Father sighed and collapsed a bit into himself. "To family, what's left of it." He sipped at his glass, the red slightly staining his lips.

I vexed my eyebrows and mussed up my hair. "Now Mara, don't do this and don't do that." I wagged my finger.

"Ha, ha," Greg said, "that's a good imitation of the Doctor."

Father leaned back in his chair. "So that's what I sound like? I only protect you for your own good. You are the most important thing in the world to me."

"I know." I kissed Father briefly and carefully on his cheek with my own wine-soaked lips.

"So Mara, what IS the most important thing to you? What would YOU like to toast to?" my father asked me.

I drank another glass of wine before I answered. "I want to look at everything with open arms. I want a sense of autobiography. Do you know what I mean?"

"Sort of," Father said.

"I don't have a clue," Greg replied.

"I think she wants more of a life," my father told Greg. "She's reached that age too soon. Everything seems to be going by so fast." His white eyebrows knitted together.

"That's a great dress," Greg acknowledged, lifting his glass.

"Father knows everything," I explained to Greg.

"Hardly," Father said. "But I know how to make something wonderful out of nothing." He winked at me. Father had never winked before. He pulled two more bottles of wine out of his suitcase.

Greg laughed. "Mara, wasn't that a television program a long time ago? Father Knows Everything," Greg looked around the room. "Hey, isn't the ball game on today?"

"I'm sorry, Greg. We don't have any TVs here. It's a silly box full of programs for stupid people," Father chided him.

Another glass of wine and I got the hiccups. My chest was warm and my stomach felt primitive, worn out. Air was compliant and pooling around my flaccid limbs. My cheeks grew flushed. I could think of the thousand ways different parts of my body had already died. I closed my eyes.

A man in a black and white suit was pouring wine into my glass from a bottle as I sat in a lounge chair. I drank it in one gulp. I tilted my feet into sandals, a long, white garment wrapped around me, hugging me, as I stood. I walked past a lit pool into darkness. I knew my way, walking down some steps, past dunes and stubby trees, and long, thin grass. A large, restless moon stared at me. I kicked off my sandals and cool sand engulfed my feet as if it wanted me to remain stationary. I entered the lapping water that spread everywhere, the cold ocean. I was searching for something underneath the waves. I kept on walking until my feet couldn't touch the bottom anymore and every part of me was leaking back into that water.

My hiccups stopped. When I opened my eyes, Father and Greg were laughing, patting each other on their backs. I had missed something although only a few minutes had whisked by. The men were blurry. A different dead chicken was slowly inching its way back up my borrowed esophagus. My insides were roiling. Father and I had studied male and female anatomy in detail so I was well versed in potential medical issues. The indiscriminate mouse was lurking under the table and began running in circles around my feet although no one seemed to notice. Maybe it was looking for food. I heard some faint howling outside, in the distance. I couldn't tell what kind of animal it was. Father grew lopsided in his chair, fell back against it, and began snoring. I didn't want to be left alone again with the guest and all that food on the table, which smelled suddenly rancid. Maybe this was the test.

"Subsumed," I yelled loudly, giving Father a good word. But he didn't wake up to receive it. "Subsumed," I repeated with as much force as I could muster. He was still snoring.

"Okay, subsumed," Greg said, his hand wavering over the table. "Calm down. Please. What the hell does it mean?"

"It's a good word, a really good word." I started crying.

"It's okay," he said. "Your father's asleep. That was a delicious wine." He tried to pat my hand across the table, but it drifted away from him, as if my new hand had a life of its own. My fingers rested on my unhappy stomach.

Then I felt my dinner knocking at my mouth, trying to get out again. I ran downstairs, to the lab, without thinking. Luckily Father had left the door unlocked when he had fetched the wine. But there wasn't a bathroom down there. I found myself vomiting around the surgery table that I knew intimately, under the watchful eyes of the Mother and Daughter in the Photographs. The Scientist looked on disinterestedly. And then I received an odd memory.

Bright lights stared at paintings which were filled with large slashes of bold colors. I said my name and all the people threaded with jewelry and beautiful, interesting clothes at the party lifted their glasses of wine to me and smiled. I, too, held a glass of wine aloft. I was happy and proud. Someone's arm slipped around my shoulders. I looked up, smiling, into the face of a handsome man. When I glanced below his waist, under his tuxedo jacket, he pawed at the floor with the legs of a black horse.

"Centaur," I yelled into the crowd.

Everyone laughed. Then I noticed everyone was dressed in elaborate costumes or they held up masks on sticks. There were cats, mice, queens, ballerinas, knights, and some people were merely dressed as themselves. I looked down at myself. I wore a smock filled with paintbrushes and splotched with paint.

"I'm so glad everyone likes my art," I told my handsome companion.

He laughed. "Who said these are your paintings?"

Greg had slipped downstairs while I wiped my mouth, drank a cup of water usually reserved for after-surgery.

"Wow, what is this place?" He was looking around.

"My father's laboratory."

"This is amazing." He started touching things, which would make Father very angry. "I'll have to ask him what he does down here."

"Please don't touch anything in here. I have to clean up." I looked at my vomit and began searching for a rag.

He sidled closer to me, closer than anyone had ever dared. "I'd rather be touching you." He took my hands into his, got onto his tiptoes, and leaned up toward my mouth.

Greg's corneas screamed with my awkward reflection, but I was looking for more than myself. I kissed Greg because I didn't care whether I hurt him or not. I wasn't afraid of him anymore. Then I couldn't remember anything else.

Chapter Three

I woke up defeated, gravel in my head, a parched throat, and stars twittering around the shrinking brain behind my eyes. I was in my own bed in my bedroom, curled into a ball under the sheets and blanket. How had I gotten there? What had happened? I was wearing my underwear, which appeared to be unmolested, and my dress lay neglected on the floor in a blue puddle. I was tucked into my bed tightly. Everything was in its usual place, dresser, chair, bed, closet. My door was unlocked and lay open like an afterthought or an invitation. I could hear birds singing outside the barred window but all their statements hurt my head. Where was Father? Greg? What had I done? The mouse scrambled behind a wall and I weakly yelled, "Shut up."

I pushed myself away from the crumpled sheets, donned the first available pants, shirt, socks and shoes and slowly made my way down the stairs. Why hadn't Father locked me in?

No one was in the kitchen or dining room although our food from last night was still there, congealing, along with our wine glasses and a half empty bottle of the infamous wine. It all smelled terrible. The living room was unchanged. No one had cleaned up and no one was there. I peeked downstairs, and the door to the laboratory was ajar.

As I crept down the stairs I saw a horrible sight: Father ladling a fresh kidney into one of his pickling jars. He had weighed it, labeled the jar. He saved everything. I knew that. An opened corpse lay on the surgical table and it was slit down the center, the skin pulled aside into two tents. Most of the cadaver's interior had already been removed. A few intestines and the complete skeletal system and peeling skin remained. I had seen pieces of carcasses around the laboratory. I didn't know where Father got these things. I saw the corpse's bare feet, hairy legs, male genitalia, the open crater of the body. I couldn't see upward from the gash of a chest under the glaring lights. I couldn't discern the face. The lights over the body hurt my eyes and I shielded them. Father was very busy, in his blue mask, gloves, and scrubs, absorbed in his work. His jacket was smeared with blood.

"Is this what I am?"

Father jumped, with a scalpel and tongs in his hands. "Shit, Mara. You scared me." I could see his bloodshot eyes. He was tired. "Did I leave the door open? Shit. Oh well."

"You left my bedroom unlocked too. That is, if it was you who put me to bed."

"Of course I did. Who else would have?" Father's eyes blinked under his eyeglasses. He pulled down his mask so he could talk. "Oh yes, well. No. I shouldn't have brought out that wine last night. But still, all in all, it was a good night. You did supremely well, Mara, except for the bit about coming down to the laboratory. I think we'll be ready for excursions soon." He smiled. "I can't wait to show you off to my colleagues, my darling daughter. Do you think you're ready?"

I nodded. But even that hurt.

"Good, maybe in about a year, maybe two, with some more social exposure, body stability, training. We could travel the world." He moved his gloved hand around in the air. "You look under the weather today. How are you feeling?"

I pointed at my head. "It aches a bit."

"Ah, yes. Wine will do that. That was your first time drinking. Take an aspirin and call me in the morning." He laughed and I didn't know why. "You should go back to bed. Do you want me to lock you back up?"

I shook my fuzzy head. "Did Greg say much about me before he left?"

Father removed his bloody elastic gloves. He looked at the floor. He said quietly, "When I woke up, I came downstairs and found Greg reading about my personal experiments in my private office. He had gotten pretty far. He knew a lot, too much. He started firing questions at me about you and the other Maras." Father went over to the Photographs, touched the Mother's face, kissed his finger and then pressed it on the Daughter. "You're too precious to lose."

I wasn't sure whether he was talking to me or the Daughter.

He continued, "He had all these ideas on how to make money from the results and what could be done with my successes, like bringing wealthy people back to life, creating replicas of famous people, allowing rich people to live forever. It was disgusting, Mara, and I couldn't listen to that moron go on and on. Besides, he was going to tell everyone. And I had already learned," he pointed to the photograph of the Scientist, "that failure made me stronger and taught me to try harder. People can make things difficult when all you want is something simple." He looked at me teary-eyed.

"I didn't hear anything going on last night. Is he coming back to visit?"

"Greg?" Father looked askance at me.

I nodded with pain.

"Who do you think is on this table?"

I shuffled to the top of the table and saw Greg's pale head. The cranium and brain had been excavated and a large slit circled his throat. The light focused on his familiar face. I began shaking and crying uncontrollably. I was horrified.

"It's immoral to kill any living creature, even if you don't mean to," I yelled, really to remind myself. Father appeared surprised and reached up to stroke the hair on my head. "I did this to him, didn't I?" I sobbed while somebody else's tears stained my father's jacket. "I'm sorry. I didn't mean to do it."

44

"Oh no, Mara, you fell asleep on top of the operating table, and I had to carry you upstairs. This happened when Greg and I were discussing my projects becoming our projects." He glanced at me skeptically. "Why, did anything else happen?"

"No," I shook my head. Was this the first time I had purposefully excluded information? "So I didn't kill him by mistake?"

"No, Mara. I killed him intentionally to stop him from saying anything and pursuing his ideas for the project. He didn't have any family or friends. Life is hard, sweetheart."

I was relieved it hadn't been me. But I was disturbed by Father. "What about death?"

"It's harder on the people around you." He tentatively probed something inside of Greg. "And Greg didn't have anyone."

I thought about what Father often told me, "If you have to think about what you've done, you didn't do it well enough." My father was everything to me. I sat on a chair and wailed some more. I didn't know if it was for my father or for me. I looked at my hands and knew I was capable, intentionally or not. I was not always aware of my accelerating strength. I peered at my distorted father through my tears. One of us always needed something. One of us loved or was being loved. That would never change. Something within me had transformed me, something that was my own.

I was beginning to understand how good and bad could live together. "What makes something alive?"

"I don't know. I only know what I can do to regenerate cells step by step. It's a long, meticulous project."

"Lugubrious," I gave my father.

"Wow," he said. "Thanks for the great word." He continued working on Greg, whose face I couldn't look at again. "I have a limited time to get some of these organs and body parts. Sorry, Mara." He peered at me over his mask. "You know that you can never talk about my work with anyone," he reiterated.

I nodded slowly. It was terrible. It was my inheritance.

"Dolorous," he gave me. If he was smiling behind his mask I couldn't see it.

♦　♦　♦　♦　♦

I slept all afternoon and that night I knew I needed to talk to Father about all the things he didn't want to talk about. I made spaghetti and spinach. My head was better, but again I wondered how many of someone else's brain cells I had killed.

I passed him a plate. "What are your plans for the future?"

"I don't know right now, Mara. I have other things on my mind."

"Is anyone going to come about Greg?"

"I told them at work that he met someone on the internet and probably left to be with her in Thailand. The police might find his skeleton in a state very far away from here in an anonymous storage facility. I'll clean out his apartment. Since he doesn't have any relatives or friends or anyone close, it should be easy." He began eating. "And I might be promoted to Greg's position as a supervisor now."

"What are you going to do with the body parts?"

Father smiled. "Why, Mara? Would you like a male companion?"

I spit out my food. "What would I do with one?"

"Would you like someone else like you?"

I thought to myself that I wouldn't do that to someone. What I said was, "No, this is enough." I pointed my fork at my father and then back at my chest. I put the fork down, cradling it. "Why am I so large and strong?"

"Your frame has to be bigger to fit everything inside. Your strength comes from the way the muscles are regenerated and attached and with my new adhesive compound you are growing stronger."

I hesitated. "Tell me about her."

"Who?" He looked at me sadly over his food.

He knew who.

"She was twenty. She was riding in the back seat of the car. My wife was in the passenger seat. Her life was just beginning." He held a spoon in his hand, but he wasn't eating. He was far away. He didn't want to talk.

"What was she like?"

"We were close. She was smart, pretty. She was thinking about becoming a scientist. She was practical yet she wrote beautifully. She was a kind person."

"Was she married or seeing anyone?" I knew this was painful for him, maybe also for me.

"No. She had several boyfriends in high school and a serious relationship early in college, but they had decided it wasn't going to become anything more and they had broken up several months before the accident." He started crying although he didn't make any noise.

"Was her name Mara?"

"I don't want to say her name."

"What happened to the other Maras?"

"Some are in you. You know that." He didn't want to speak anymore.

He had invented me. I wanted to leave him something. "Thank you for creating me," I told him and kissed his wet cheek. But when I picked up my fork I realized I had bent it again.

◆　◆　◆　◆　◆

The fork had given me an idea. I went to my bedroom window that night, brushed the curtains aside, began pressing the bars with all my strength. They started to bend. I could hear metal groaning. I stopped. I could see the moon and trees swaying in an evening breeze through the space between the bars. I received another memory.

I was in a prison, painted shades of gray and green, and a woman in a uniform handed me a flute. She locked the door, comprised of vertical bars, behind her after she entered. I was alone on a cot with a dark gray blanket. I could feel a deep melancholy returning. Photographs of smiling men, women, and children lined the cement walls. I lifted that flute to my lips, my blonde hair fell around my neck and flowed around the instrument. Music wafted between those bars, roamed everywhere.

The woman in the uniform smiled, said, "Would you rather be a musician or a criminal?"

I didn't need to answer. I thought: the criminal could kill the musician. What could the musician do but play? So I did. That music was a happy maelstrom let loose upon that tiny place. I played until I forgot where I was.

I was sitting on my own bed, smiling. It was morning. Sun stained the floor. A trapezoid of light, the shape of my barred window, was draped against the locked door. Evening was approaching later and later, which meant it was summer. I could see Father's car, parked as usual, a bit down the road, near another road. I had never been outside. This house, Father, the computer, and books were the only ways I could view the world. I had other people's memories to learn from too. What was he saving me for?

I removed my left sock and studied the space where the top of my big toe had been. I was worried about cellular degeneration. I pondered the shape of Greg's big toe. Father would fix it if I let him. It would mean acquiring more parts, more operations, just to maintain me. I knew Father wouldn't be content until he could make a Mara as close to his Daughter as possible. I wasn't that Mara. I also knew that I had to create my own memories; otherwise other people's would overtake me. The outrageous mouse ran to the middle of my room, had the nerve to creep up to the sock near my foot. The mouse's whiskers twitched as it smelled my sock. Then it gingerly put the sock in its mouth and ran underneath my bed.

"Aren't you afraid of me?" I laughed. "You should be," I told the unruly mouse. "Recalcitrant," I loudly gave the hidden mouse. "And what are you going to do with my sock?"

What had happened to the others? Had any of them escaped? Were they all within me now? What was out there? Books described the complexity, the layers, but could the world, which encompassed everything, be worse than living with an affectionate murderer? I wanted to abandon my original sin. I wanted the world and I needed provisions.

I stared at my perplexing mirror, although I had come to believe I finally understood it. I did, finally, resemble the Daughter although I was more angular, bumpy and slightly scarred. I could pass muster. I smiled and moved my head and saw dark hair, brown eyes, long eyelashes, Father's animated eyebrows, the new mole. I was what Father had made.

I rose, finished bending the bars on my window. The metal bent more easily, complaining more quietly and steadily, paint and chips of wood littered the sill. I whispered a song I didn't know, that perhaps I had acquired through a memory. It was about the fate of a beautiful woman. It didn't end well. My voice was raspy, too rough and uncertain. I was afraid. I sat and wrote to calm myself.

The Story of Hearing

An abandoned child lived alone among animals that had briefly climbed into themselves for the winter. The animals found her shivering behind a rock when they were following some ants one day. The girl had a good life among the animals, howling occasionally, imitating them, when food or a place to sleep couldn't be found. She liked all the tiny lives around her. One day she found a book dropped in a field, and she remembered how to read. She wanted words for how she lived. She discovered "hibernation" and "unreliable." The girl recited phrases from the rotting book, hoping something would happen.

49

She said one sentence out loud, "A nervous wolf barks over unused bodies."

Something twisted inside the animals. They left the girl because she had become too different from them. All they saw in the book was marks on a page. When they were gone, the girl began to listen to silence, the trees, leaves rustling, a river splashing, flowers unfurling, bushes brushing against one another. "Tentative." She danced, remembering human movement. She banged on some stones with a stick and began singing tunes that leaped into her head. The songs had places to go. And all the curious animals returned.

I slipped my new story into one of my books. Then I sang to the mouse about places I had never been, Kentucky, New York, Seattle, Los Angeles. I closed my eyes and saw postcards stuck on a vanity mirror. They were from France, Italy, England, the pictures were cracked and peeling. I couldn't read the names, addresses, or messages. They were surrounded by medals and ribbons. I opened my eyes. I stuck the top of my head outside my window and felt air from the world combing my hair. I shook my hair until it smelled of cut grass, roses growing up a trellis, new leaves, car exhaust, fading sunlight. I heard someone honk a car horn, a dog whine, a child's loud protest in the far distance, beckoning. I shut the curtains.

"What do you think?" I asked the now quiet mouse under my bed. "Should we make a break for it when it's dark?"

There wasn't any answer.

◆　◆　◆　◆　◆

I leaped out the window in the middle of the night, under a full moon. I had left behind my books, stories, computer, clothes, Father, and the house, which was everything I knew. I scooped up that ornery mouse, placed it in the pocket of my shirt, my sock stuffed around it. I landed with a thud in the dirt and grass from the second story window. Another toe had bent and broken off in the jump. I could feel it roaming in my sock and shoe. I kicked my foot. I didn't have time to inspect it. But losing body parts didn't hurt much. It was as if my body was rejecting them. However, operations to fix the parts did. I was on the ground on my hands and knees, and the mouse grew frightened and hurled itself out of my pocket.

"Oh," I mumbled toward my escaping companion.

That was when I looked into yellow eyes with a start. More of her came into view when she snatched the mouse from right in front of me. It was one version of Gloves. She had obviously also been losing body parts. Whether it was to cellular degeneration or fights or other predators I would never know. She had most of her gray fur, one ear, a partial tail. She had lost several toes.

"Gloves," I murmured sweetly at her.

She looked into my eyes, the mouse in her mouth, and she trotted away with her prize.

I reached out for her, called her again. But her body vanished into a thicket of trees under the luminescent moon. I wanted to go with her. Maybe we could scavenge and hunt together, learn each other's language, help one another. I knew tonight was my only chance. If I didn't leave immediately, Father would come after me. He probably wouldn't call the police. It would be too risky. But there were detectives and people he could pay to locate me and bring me home. It depended on how much I truly meant to him. How valuable was I really? Maybe the next Mara would be better. He could correct his mistakes.

I thought of Humbert Humbert, toward the end of *Lolita*, "This then is my story. It has bits of marrow sticking to it, and blood, and beautiful bright-green flies. At this or that twist of it I feel my slippery self eluding me, gliding into deeper and darker waters than I care to probe." He ended the book mentioning the refuge of art and the story being their only piece of immortality, he and Lolita, his pseudo-daughter. There was still much I didn't understand about that book.

I ran back toward the house although I was afraid. I limped slightly until I adjusted to the loss of another toe. Front door or window? I decided on the window. It was quieter. I bent those bars, removed my shirt and broke the glass, catching shards in my empty pants on the sill. I slowly tiptoed back through the living room until I found the car keys, $110, and some food from the refrigerator.

I left Father a note which said, "I love you always and have failed you for the last time. Don't look for me. Mara Six will be exuberant."

I could have stayed then, apologized. But I didn't. I slipped back out that window stealthily, shook out my clothes, filled them again.

Part II

The Forest

Chapter Four

I pushed Father's car until it was far enough away from the house, approaching the road that was invisible at the far edge of the forest that encapsulated our house. It was dark out, but I could see, finally, what was beyond us. A well-structured road cut like a ribbon right through all those trees. It would go somewhere. I sat for a moment on the white hood of Father's car. I could smell grass, trees, warm air, Gloves nearby, the dead mouse, cigarette smoke, grease, and moonlight. Moonlight's scent was cool and lightweight like a melon.

I whispered a short conversation in the direction of some tree leaves. I had to leave soon. "Goodbye Gloves. Goodbye Father."

I listened to the breeze. An alarm sounded in the distance, then voices. I could feel every muscle in my body alert and waiting, ready.

"I don't know where I am. I don't know where I'm going." I suddenly thought of *Crime and Punishment* and realized I hadn't understood that book before.

Then I received a memory of my arms and legs locked in chains, my red hair whipping my face. I was dressed in black leather. Some of my body parts were pierced with jewelry and scribbled with pictures. Something punctured my nose. I was screaming instructions, and I hurt. It was a funny feeling that I didn't understand but I wasn't scared or anxious. I was . . . interested.

I pushed a little harder and the car rolled onto the road. I unlocked it and folded my height inside. I tried to remember the car manual I had once read out of boredom. When I inserted the key, the engine began. I liked the interior of the car, having only seen it from the exterior. It was roomy and Father's odor still lingered along with a sharp, bitter, medical smell. Bushes kicked the side windows, trees sprouted into the rear window, and I uprooted some grass and dirt with the tires, then the car returned to its correct lane. Insects pummeled the windshield. Stars blinked and the moon changed its position. I went slowly at first, then sparse houses appeared, a few at a time, stunned with electric lights. Several cars passed me as my car jerked, but not many. I wanted to stop and study the passengers, my fellow world travelers. I had so many questions. I wanted to know so much. I wished I could have brought Gloves or that mouse along. Then I discovered the radio. I was ecstatic. I alternated between rock and roll, talking, and classical music.

I decided to write about myself: *The Adventures of Mara Five.* I had read books. I wished to record what I learned. "Precarious," I gave myself. I thought further, "Persistent."

Had my father donated a part of himself to me at some time, a fingernail or strand of hair or an ear component? I could suddenly see myself through his eyes: a still incomplete, dark girl/woman with a kind enough heart, some intellectual skills, a patchwork body, tall, with too much strength, who launched herself into the unknown for no reason he could fathom. Father would say that death is a part of life but too much death had changed Father. I shivered from both fright and my own excitement. Father would want me to record what happened to me so that he could, maybe, prevent Mara Six from enacting the same mistakes. I had begun my own experiment without him.

A sign pointed toward a Rest Area. I needed rest. I turned and parked near two stray cars under lamplights. There was a lit sign for BATHROOMS nearby. I sensed trees like tangled veins twining all around me. I had a sweater decorated with flowers that I wrapped tightly around me. I didn't have any other clothes besides the pants and shirt I'd been wearing when I left. The moon seemed large and round and made a noise that reminded me of someone being surprised in a cartoon, saying Oh. I addressed it through my windshield, "Accommodation."

An older woman, wearing a scarf, a yellow dress, and shoes with thick, rubber bottoms was walking a small, beige dog through a path near the bathrooms. I had never seen a living older woman or a dog before except in pictures. She saw me staring and waved at me. I waved back. It was my first interaction in the wide world. The dog barked so I twisted the dial of the radio and the speaker filling with jazz grew louder. The music made me think of Father frying eggs, my favorite, in the morning, while I recited the various constellations and their properties. I could feel the stars in their movements, swarming above my head, over the roof of the car.

I retrieved the bag with my wilted, forlorn food, a soggy cheese sandwich, some drooping lettuce. I ate. The older woman and dog left in a large car that resembled a kitchen appliance. I was a conglomeration of bones, and skin, and body parts. I needed a plan, a purpose. I would prove myself. I would send Father postcards with descriptions of my adventures. The music was full of answers. I allowed it to travel through me as I lay down on the car seat, inhaling what was left of Father's scent. I fell asleep.

I awoke very early in the morning. The moon, that inevitable planet, was fading, and the sun rose over a landscape that resembled a body's outline on a table. A red light began to spread through tree branches, a lung's inflation behind ribs. The ground suggested muscles. Houses across the road, teeth. It was incredibly beautiful. I wasn't lonely. I could turn on the radio whenever I wanted. I could do whatever I wanted.

I needed to go to the bathroom. The rest area was almost completely empty. The bathroom was all steel and concrete. No one else was in there, so I washed up. When I splashed water on my healed face below the disgruntled mirror, I understood what my purpose was.

I would become my own creation.

I left the bathroom slightly dazed. It was up to me. A boy/man around my age stood outside smoking a cigarette, which smelled sweet and used up, and I thought of the color black. His hair was pulled back in a ponytail, and he wore an animal skin jacket and a large, felt hat. A long, feather earring dangled from his left ear. I sat on the edge of the sidewalk, removed my shoe, surreptitiously pulled out my toe.

"What state is this?" I asked him.

He looked at me askance. "Montana." He surveyed the parking lot. "Your license plate is from Montana," he said gently. I hadn't noticed the car plate. He pointed to his left. "That way is Seattle. That's where I'm going." He nodded at his car.

"Do you have a needle and thread?" I wanted to try sewing my toe back on.

"I can't say that I do." He inhaled, and curlicues of smoke coiled into the air from his mouth.

I slipped my toe into my pants pocket so he wouldn't notice it. I should have been more prepared. I could have planned a bit better. "Would you like to have my car?" I asked him.

He stepped back further from me. "No. I came in my own car. Otherwise I wouldn't be at a rest area. Why? Is there something wrong with it?" He vexed his eyebrows but he didn't look like Father.

"No," I laughed. I wondered if the police would come. Or if Father would even call them when he discovered I was missing.

The man was still smoking his cigarette. A brown wispy earring dripped from his left ear. "Are you from around here?"

"Yes, I think so." A few more cars entered the parking area. "Have you been to many places?" I suddenly thought about eating a country, tasting it. It would be dust, spices, language, a food that was sharp like cheese.

Then I had a memory of a large storm brewing overhead. Dark clouds filled up the sky, which smelled of sulphur, rain, and a rancid soup. I was a woman scientist in a foreign country. I ran underground to some kind of enormous laboratory. I recognized microscopes, test tubes, glass bottles, slides, droppers, sheaves of paper with different numbers and letters, various instruments, and machines, more machines than I'd seen before. But there weren't any body parts, only jars filled with red, green, blue liquids. Masks, a breathing apparatus, thick body suits were strewn on the floor. I barked to someone I couldn't see, telling them to do something quickly. Then the storm began to batter the outside entrance, the windows. I thought about being somewhere else, another country, and then the memory stopped abruptly.

The man had been talking; ". . . so that's where I've been." He seemed lonely, like me.

I hoped my body would sort itself out, become what it would, but I was beginning to worry about my mind and all those unsorted memories. "Profound."

"Thank you," the man said, appropriately. He sat down next to me on the cement edge, his cigarette a smudge under his foot. Trees undulated, leaves winked in the light; as the sun grew higher more cars were arriving. "What's your name?"

"Mara."

"Mine's Carl." He extended his hand. I shook it a little too vigorously. He waved his arm in the air, surveyed the parking lot. "I better be going, Mara. It's getting late."

"Can I go with you, Carl?" I hastily put my shoes back on and stood, brushing off my clothes.

"Um," he looked up at me. "You're a tall one."

"I can help with the driving." I sensed his hesitancy.

"I have a dog." He rubbed his arm.

"I've never met a dog." He looked at me strangely. I believed our conversation was going well. I gathered my food and threw the clanging car keys onto the hood of Father's old white Ford.

"Her name is Berserk."

"Ha, ha. Good name." My abrading laugh seemed to bother him.

"Now why are you leaving your car?" He appeared concerned. He fiddled with his earring.

"It's from another life. I need to fill myself up with new experiences."

"Like what?"

We were walking to his car, an old Dodge Omni with peeling blue paint. I wondered how my new body parts could be integrated so well when I had already lost two toes, regeneration hand in hand with degeneration. Maybe it was Father's adhesive concoction. The dog was bigger than Gloves and jumped from seat to seat, barking, when it saw us. It had longer fur and was clumsier, not using its toes. "Music unfurls inside of me. It's like talking to someone deep within me. Only the person's also tickling my skin to get out."

He opened the car door. "Step in," he said, frowning.

A whirlwind of fur greeted me, leaping, licking my hand. No creature had been so happy to see me before, except maybe Father, if I was looking particularly good that day. I smiled at the excitable creature. I compacted myself into the passenger seat.

"She's a good girl." Carl slid into the driver's seat, petting his dog. "Friendly."

"Do you have any children?"

"None that I know of. Do you?"

I laughed at that. It was a harsh noise. "I don't think I can."

"You're amenable."

"Thanks for the word." But I thought: ambiguous.

He began driving as houses, trees, other cars, and people flew by us. Berserk settled down in the back seat. I had a chance to study the dog, which alternated between being restless and comfortable. She would lie down, then stand and circle the same spot and ease into it again. She had light blue eyes and white and brownish long silky-looking fur. I didn't want to touch her, afraid I might hurt her. As we moved further and further away from Father and my whole life, I felt a longing for what I used to be, embedded deep inside of me. Childcloud. A return to someone who didn't exist anymore, like a ghost who remained immobile, haunting only one house.

"What do you do?" He was watching the road.

"I'm here with you and Berserk."

"No, I mean, what do you usually do with yourself all day long?"

"I read mostly, in my living quarters. Or I had operations. But I don't know what I'll be doing now." His profile resembled Greg's a little. "Why? What do you do with yourself?"

"I make log homes and I'm in a country western band called 'Where Do We Go from Here?'" He smiled. "I'll play you some of our music in a while. It's just that Berserk sings along with the songs."

I suddenly remembered a tiny white bird that perched on my window sill and sang until there weren't any more sad thoughts in my head. It shivered and flapped its wings and made me happy. Trees from the forest, spruce, pine, fir, juniper, filled up the rest of my window. I wasn't sure whether this was my own memory or someone else's.

"Is this small talk?" I inquired as I lay my head back against the seat. I was relaxed although I had absolutely no idea where I was going, away from everything I knew.

I missed my blue dress for a moment. The old was receding in the small strange car mirrors and the new was constantly surprising in the windshield. I saw fat people, children, animals roaming within fences, outdoor movie theatres, irregularly shaped lawns, factories, bowling alleys, churches, clothes stores, a black cat, furniture displayed in someone's yard. It was all new to me. Everything was so alive, always moving and changing.

"Yes," he sputtered. "I guess this is small talk."

"Do you know any stories?"

"Yes, but first I need to let Berserk out."

The dog knew what he was saying because she crawled into my lap, began whining, and poked her nose against the glass, leaving sprays of mucus on the side window. I petted her brown and white freckled fur, her floppy ears rising and falling, silky and smooth.

"I know, I know, but this is I90 and it's hard to stop," Carl said to Berserk.

"She likes you," he said to me, which worried me since caring for another creature usually didn't turn out well.

"What do you think it would be like to have fur?"

"Warm," he said, parking the car in a jut by the side of the road. A sign up ahead said, WELCOME TO IDAHO. He opened my door and Berserk ran quickly and deeply into the woods, which swallowed her up completely so there was no trace of her, except maybe her paw prints in the underbrush.

"How far did you want to go?" He stood along the edge of the road near my door.

"I don't know yet." I unfolded myself from the car. "But I'll tell you when I've arrived."

"How will you know you're there?" He was smoking a cigarette, the fumes wafting in every direction, unsure of their final destinations.

Some of the smoke clothed me, coiling around me, and I coughed.

"Sorry," he said and turned away.

Just then Berserk ran out from the woods and crossed in front of the car. I ran after her into the fast, oncoming traffic. She froze just as a car tried to halt right in front of her, braking loudly, skidding slowly. I grabbed the front bumper, raised the warm metal car, pushed it back slightly onto its back wheels and then I lifted it from underneath. My muscles tensed, my back arched, and I heard a cracking noise from somewhere in my hands. I tossed it backwards several feet quickly and without thinking. I hadn't known before that I had that much strength. Father's strange chemicals at their peak or adrenaline or both? Cars behind the first one tried to stop; some were successful and some weren't. The collisions were noisy and continuous. I could see two children's faces in the back seat inside the car I had thrown, a boy and a small girl. They were shocked, their arms thrown around one another. The driver, a man, was alarmed, his hands tightly clutching the useless steering wheel. The back of the bronze-colored car crumpled as it landed, the people inside were jostled but unharmed. Berserk was now stationary and shivering, staring at all the damage done so quickly. She looked at me, cried, and then ran back to Carl, who was shouting something and waving his hands at her from the side of the road. He kneeled to ruffle her fur and grab her.

I had lost the top half of my left finger, which lay near my feet on the highway. I retrieved it and tossed the finger piece into my pocket. Carl was crying as he locked Berserk in the back of the car. I ran to them.

"Those poor people. There were about twelve cars involved. All the others passed by slowly, gawking at everything. Everyone looks okay though," Carl said surveying the scene his head rotating. He turned toward me. "Thank you, thank you so much for saving her life," he said. "She means everything to me. She must have been running from something. How did you do that?" He looked me up and down, "What are you?"

I smiled. I had saved an animal, for once. My heart was agitated and pumping loudly, blood seemed to course through me in waves. I was drenched in sweat and oddly excited and exhausted. Upset people began swarming out of their cars and coming toward us. I scanned the accident and I could see that no one was hurt, just their cars. There were too many people hurrying toward me with clenched and hurling fists or hands on their cheeks or in their hair, and they frightened me. They were shouting questions and statements in my direction, "What the hell happened?" "All this for a damned dog!" "Who are you?" "How did you do that?"

"Resonance," I gave Carl before grabbing my food sack from the back of his car, and quickly petting Berserk, who licked my hand. I rushed deep into the woods the terrified dog had just abandoned.

♦　♦　♦　♦　♦

I returned to isolation, in the forest, but this time it was my choice. The wide, wide world was confusing. I couldn't imagine walking down streets full of people, some staring at me, or trying to sit in a tiny chair in a restaurant or inside of someone's house, and having only part of me fitting in it. I would have to stoop for doorways (Father had adjusted ours for a Mara a long time ago), eat miniature food, cram myself into subways or taxis or buses. And I would be afraid of harming someone with the accidental swat of my hand since people and objects were so close in a city. I didn't want to live in a tiny box of an apartment stacked upon a hive of other similar ones. It wouldn't have worked. That was my personal hypothesis.

I brushed past trees, bushes, hurrying. I stomped on grass, hard earth, flattened moss, ferns, and the timidly unfurling flowers. I could hear a crowd following me. After a short time it thinned out.

A woman said, "I don't know where she went. And what would we do if we caught up with her anyway?"

A man's voice answered, "I don't know but I sure want more information than that stupid guy with his dog could give us. Mara. It's probably a fake name. I can't believe she did all that."

An older man said, "Yeah, she's responsible. Wrecking those cars has consequences."

"She was amazing," a tired, young woman uttered. "But fuck it. Who knows where she went out here. And it'll be getting dark soon."

Then, after some time, I couldn't hear any voices or footsteps anymore. I was in a valley, and evening stained the sky. An ethereal outline of the moon appeared. I wanted peace. I wanted time and experiences to ponder.

I gathered wood, rubbed logs together easily, made a nice fire. I ate what was left of some apples and lettuce, broccoli, potatoes. I wasn't cold. I checked my skin, but there weren't any scratches, abrasions, or cuts. The skin near my newest right hand was a bit frayed and overworked. I would try to rest it, so it wouldn't come undone. My heart was still racing. All the rest of my inner circuitry seemed to be humming along just fine. Nothing else had broken. I missed that dog, Berserk, and Gloves too. I could hear a howling around me and the crackle of sticks underneath delicate, careful paws. A flurry of birds quieted with the oncoming night. There was the sharp cry of a surprised rodent, rustling leaves in a breeze, grass flapping onto grass. I could hear water moving in the distance and a synchronic hum to the air that contained all the noises. Although the animals tried to be silent, tried to creep up on their prey, tiny noises revealed them. The fire imitated bones cracking and sputtering at intervals. The symphony of sounds, beyond, out in the forest, was my new house.

Odors were masked by the smoldering of the fire, except for the darkening, damp earth underneath where I lay. Cinders rose in the air and flew off. Sparks crackled and broke apart. In the darkness I stayed in the circle of light. I could feel the forest stretching in every direction, and I felt free and luxurious.

"Unencumbered," I gave to the blazing light. I spread out on the ground. Far, far away was the tiniest buzz of traffic. I could hear a rush of water in the distance that nearly covered it up. I thought that every time I filled my heart with a person or animal something broke it. Bad things happened.

I sensed a light somewhere, but it was motionless, harmless, and distant. I would explore in the morning. I fell asleep, more comfortable among trees than people. The trees were less complicated.

I didn't need to explain myself or keep Father's secrets. I didn't need to worry about etiquette or about being misunderstood. I liked people; it just hadn't worked out in their favor so far.

I fell asleep, dreamed I was surrounded by cats and dogs. I petted them, nuzzled their fur with my nose. They told me stories about their lives and their owners, how they were allowed to do only this or that, restricted. How they were scolded for actions they were compelled to do, by their very nature. They complained, "What did they think I would do when they brought me here?" I liked their musty odor, honesty, grace, lack of manners. I lay myself down among them, allowed their furry hind legs, tails, paws, and heads to cover me like a big, warm, patchwork blanket. As they individually awoke, they each took a piece of me softly between their teeth and left. Finally there was nothing left of me.

I awoke with a start, the sun blinking behind trees. My fire was out, a tiny spark flashed at the center. I was certain that my dream had not been someone else's. Then I heard dogs and people. Police were arriving with flashlights, although sunlight was beginning to seep in everywhere.

They spoke to one another and to a person somewhere else through devices on their clothing. "We're pretty far into the woods and we're losing her footprints. I don't know if it's worth pursuing. She's got to come out sometime. According to the eyewitnesses, you can't miss her. I say we give up the search."

Another man's voice said, "There's an abandoned fire further on. I'll check it out. After that I say we move on to another case. She didn't harm anyone anyway."

"Roger that."

I stomped on the fire with the men's shoes Father had bought me. I grabbed two cans out of my food sack and tucked them into my sweater pockets. I ran as quickly and quietly as I could. I stopped when I reached a river that was muttering. I was panting and the noise covered up the sound from my lungs. I climbed a large tree, brushing the thin branches and leaves aside so I could sit between some of the larger limbs and watch the men. Two disturbed birds flew off. Then some bright lights roamed around my head and a woman was laughing. It wasn't really a memory. More like an aftereffect or ripples from one. I held on tight to the tree. The tree walked, with me high and hidden in its leaves. It swayed, but didn't knock me loose. Colors swirled around me.

Two men stood over my old fire. They poked it with a stick, lifted my old food bag, searching through it.

"I see her shoe prints going off that way into the deep forest." One man pointed and walked to the pile of freshly squashed bushes. "But then I lose her tracks. We could search around that way." He pointed towards the tree where I was still unseen.

"Naw, I don't want to hassle with the whole thing. Nobody's filed anything against her. People are just curious . . . and riled up. Insurance companies will handle the whole thing. It's all property damage. Let's go get some breakfast."

"Roger that." They left.

I sighed with relief and rubbed my eyes, full of a heat that emanated out of my closed lids. When I opened them the tree and I were back where we had started, near the river. I felt for my detached body parts and threw my dry toe and fingertip into the river. A fish surfaced and nibbled the top of a fingernail before the toe and finger sank, disappearing into the moving water. I had waited too long to reattach them. I knew that much from Father, who would have been concerned about my senses becoming jumbled and my loss of body parts, who would have wanted to examine me for problems and malfunctions. And, maybe, he could have fixed me. Maybe I was simply stressed, or aging, in the way my own kind did. I couldn't stand any more operations. I would rather fall apart.

"Dissembling," I whispered to my invisible extremities, to the rushing river that wore down or took apart everything in its path.

Chapter Five

And then I spotted it from the treetop, a small roughly log-hewn church. The door facing me slammed shut. Smoke began writhing from a chimney on the roof, near a simple wooden cross. I hadn't seen who had gone inside. Large evergreens weaved around the edges of the structure, obscuring the church. I had seen pictures of gold trimmed, elaborate churches whose famous spires reached high into the sky, but never one thrown together like this one. Something bubbled from my nose. When I wiped it with my hand, patches of blood spread onto my fingers. I wiped it again and it was already dry. I crept down from my tree. I crawled to one of the plain, small windows and peered inside, wondering if I would see God or one of His creators.

The interior was dark and small, with pews for about twenty people, a wood stove, and a platform, a podium, and a cross all made of wood. I concentrated on movement and finally noticed a woman with dark hair covered by a scarf bent over, washing the floor. She wore a large brown apron over a skirt, and a long sleeved blouse. Her arms repeated wide circular motions. I tiptoed to the second window on the side of the church to get a better view of her, but when I looked again, she was gone, her bucket and rag waiting on the floor. My head shifted, searching for her. Suddenly she popped up in front of me, on the other side of the cramped window, a doughy face with lines, flaring eyebrows, wide eyes the color of a summer sky.

"Boo," she said through the thin glass. "Who are you?"

"I'm Mara." Our lips moved like fish under water. I suddenly thought of *To Kill a Mockingbird*. My senses jumbled as I whispered the name of the book. I saw her face again, huge and close to mine. "If I'm Boo then who's Scout?" I asked. Her features disassembled, poured over me. Light tangled around us, bounced away from the glass, into my eyes. Stones fled and reappeared as birds all around me. Clouds were interrupting my thoughts. I licked sunlight from my lips and tasted warmth and a sweetness that resembled sugar.

"Did you say you're scouting? I haven't seen any mockingbirds and I sure haven't killed any." Her lips were moving and the church rattled. The building spilled too much light and the trees scattered.

I almost asked her where Father was. Atticus? What had he done lately to make people angry, besides me and the other Maras? What was it about fathers? The cobwebs in my mind broke, flew away, and I wove myself back together. I was standing in front of the window of the church, a woman speaking to me. It was hard for us to understand one another through the glass.

"What are you doing out here? What do you want?" Her hands gestured, a wet rag flailed in one of them. She looked cross.

"Is God inside?" I asked.

"Sometimes," she said mysteriously.

"What does it depend on?"

She smiled, disappeared from my sight. She reappeared at the door, left it open. She studied me.

"You're not one of those back-to-nature druggie hikers?" She shielded her eyes, evaluating my height and width.

I shook my head. Although I wasn't sure what she was talking about, I wasn't a hiker.

"Are you a Survivalist?"

I shook my head. I didn't think so. I wasn't really sure what I was.

"Are you carrying any weapons?" She was staring at my pants.

"No, I don't have any." I scooped out my pants pockets. "I have two cans of food." I showed them to her.

"You look big-boned, tall. You'd probably be pretty if you got cleaned up. Like my daughter. She loves these woods. She could play out here all day long. Are you from around here?"

"No, I don't think so."

"Are you running away from something?"

"Yes."

"You don't have to tell me what it is yet." She looked around, breathed deeply. "Does your mother know you're here?"

"I always wanted a mother but Father and I couldn't afford one."

She laughed. "You're a funny one." She shook her head. "Kids today."

"I'm not a Childcloud anymore."

"That's what they all say." She peered at me closely. "That's an odd way to put it." She brushed her dirty hands. "Well, you can come inside while I work. Then I could probably find a little food or something for you. We don't get many visitors here."

She motioned for me to follow her inside the church. I stooped to pass underneath the doorway but found the inside roomier than it had appeared from outside. It had high ceilings so I could stand tall and stretch out my arms. The large room inside was simple, wooden, and clean. Quilts with stories decorated the walls and seats.

The woman knelt again, dipping her rag into the soapy water. She scrubbed the floor in front of the podium tiredly. "My name's Theresa. My husband used to lead the services here, when he wasn't out hunting or fishing. That was before a bear got him. I get paid to keep it clean in here. I also take in wash to help make ends meet." She liked to talk to the rhythm of her cleaning. She stood and her knees creaked. "My little girl, Kat, short for Katrina, she's ten now and can hardly remember her father. She's growing up to be a wild little thing." She laughed. "I guess I was pretty wild too, a long time ago, but there isn't much of a town left out here anymore. All the kids want to move to the city." Her hand flew to her mouth. "I'm going on and on. Can I get you some water or some crackers and cheese to eat?"

"Yes. Please," I remembered to say.

When she left for another room, tucked off somewhere in the tiny church, I fell to the floor and continued her washing. I was weary and hungry but I, too, liked the way the movement of my hands matched my thoughts. I decided that the body had its own trajectory and rhythms and there was nothing I could do about it.

"Tautology," I whispered to myself.

Theresa returned with yellow cheese and brown crackers on a white plate and a big glass of milk. She set them down on a pew. "You're missing part of your finger," and she pointed at my left hand, "but I can't believe how much work you've done in the short time I was gone."

I glanced at her astonished face. "I'm happy to help." I knew I couldn't maim the floor no matter how hard I scrubbed.

"You're a strong girl." Her features collapsed into thought, making her wrinkles more apparent. "Go eat. Go on."

I went to the food and gobbled it down. "Thank you." I wiped my mouth with my sleeve. I was glad that Father had taught me etiquette among humans. The woman watched me the whole time.

"I can see that you have some tiny scars along your wrists and elsewhere." She shook her head. "You can tell me about anything bothering you when you feel ready. Now, do you have any place to go?"

I shook my head, glanced at the drying floor. "Is God hiding from us?"

"Mara, Honey," she said patiently, "He's all around us. Can't you feel Him?" She closed her eyes.

I shook my head, but she didn't see. I closed my eyes too and a memory developed.

I was a little girl in bed at night. My mother, who spoke a language I didn't recognize, snuggled me deeper into my blankets. Her words were soft yet measured. I was afraid of the oncoming darkness, and I wanted to fling my arms around her, hold her to me, keep her with me for protection. But I didn't. I was brave and said goodnight in that strange language. I thought about stiff robots stealing me away and carnivorous plants growing closer and closer to me while I innocently slept. So I stayed awake the entire night. At dawn, sunlight flooding my room, a large, dark silhouette crept along my bedroom door. Just as I was going to scream an enormous man's hand clapped itself over my mouth, silencing me.

"Whenever you're done praying," Theresa was saying, "I'll finish up the seats. Then you can come and stay with us a little while. You can get cleaned up and eat some more food." She reached for her rags.

I grabbed her bucket and rags, nearly toppling Theresa. I finished the pews. I sat on the stage with the podium, near the stove, and the crudely carved statue of a man hung from the wall. His traumatized eyes were painted blue and bore into the back of my head, which was what I imagined thrombosis felt like. I wanted to rest.

She dampened the fire. "Okay, I'll show you the way home, Mara."

"Superfluous," I gave her. But she didn't respond. "Munificent," I tried. She peered at me strangely. Maybe she didn't appreciate the new words.

"No booze or drugs or anything like that is allowed in my house." She stuffed her cleaning sack away, stared at me.

"I didn't like wine when I tried it once. And I don't want any more operations," I responded. "That's why I'm here."

She looked at me sadly. She placed a calloused palm at my neck and steered me toward the church door. I would need time to make sense of my worldly experiences so far. I didn't always comprehend them. Theresa was the first mother I had ever met and, so far, she was very different from Father.

♦   ♦   ♦   ♦   ♦

A narrow path wound through the forest. I couldn't discern it, but Theresa knew it well. Trees nodded at us, bushes yielded, rocks crouched among the prehistoric ferns and gangly flowers. I could hear the confessions of mice along vanishing points. Colors compressed and expanded in front of my eyes, but I suspected it wasn't real, only my senses jumbling again. I heard water hurrying somewhere, alongside our route. I wanted to poke my finger through the latticed sky. Instead I tried to concentrate on following Theresa's footsteps. I wished Gloves was following us, rendering mouse bodies. One life opened into others. I, too, was replaceable.

"Aberration," I whispered to myself.

After over an hour of walking, Theresa pointed to a tiny weed-choked house that was barely visible. A Childcloud with fragile sticks for arms and legs, a spasm of blonde hair, a brown sack dress, and eyes that resembled white clouds ran out, across the yard, toward us. Her eyelids were open, but I couldn't see her eyes.

"Who's with you, Mother?" she screamed at Theresa. "I hear other footsteps, heavy ones, and somebody breathing."

"She's been blind since birth," Theresa explained to me.

The girl bounded closer. I could smell dirt, baby powder, chewing gum, oily hair, and something sweet like cherry lollipops. I moved my tongue around inside my mouth, oranges too. I could almost taste the little girl. She reached out toward my waist, but I didn't want her to touch me. I moved backwards.

"Kat, this is Mara. She'll be staying with us for a little while."

"Why?" the girl spat out nastily. She was a whirlpool.

"She doesn't have any other place to go and she can help me with work." Theresa moved toward the house but Kat blocked her.

"We don't need her." The little girl had a big voice. "I can smell her from here."

"What do I smell like?" I asked the frightening creature. I was curious. I was both afraid of her and afraid of hurting her.

"The inside of a balloon." She was a smudge against the landscape.

"Yes, well, Mara needs a bath. And you probably do too, Miss Katrina." Theresa reached for the little girl's neck to guide her toward the house, but at her mother's touch the girl burst away from her. She faced away, expertly, just before hitting a pine tree. I had never seen a blind girl before.

Theresa and I continued to the house. An airplane overhead ripped the sky open without apologizing. It left a white trail, sky scars. I was weary and corroding. Inside were four small rooms and everything was made of wood. I had to accommodate my body to the lower ceilings and doors. Theresa showed me around. A fireplace, stove, big wash tub, table and a few chairs in one, a bathroom with another older steel tub, two bedrooms, the larger one had a wooden cross over the bed like at the church.

"My husband made almost everything here, including the house. He made the table and chairs. You can stay in Kat's room for now. She can sleep with me."

The little girl was in the corner seething, muttering something under her breath. I began to speak in colors, another conflagration of my senses. "I don't need the red. I can sleep in the white." I pointed incoherently to the kitchen area.

"Come," Theresa said, "you're too tired. Sleep. Then we can wash and eat." She showed me into the girl's bedroom. When we realized the bed was too small for me, we took the sheets and blankets and put them on the floor. I barely fit inside the room. Theresa closed the curtains and left. Before I slept I could hear them arguing.

"I want Miss Moscovitz and my ball," the girl whined. I wondered how I had sounded to Father.

"Come here, Kat. It's only for a little while. Don't worry. We'll get Miss Moscovitz and your ball tomorrow."

"But I don't like it! I don't like her."

In the remaining dim light of the room, I saw a yellow ball with absurd black stripes and a half-naked plastic doll with part of a dress and a hurricane of blonde hair. The doll was missing an arm and a chunk of her thigh, and she was covered in scratches. I understood Miss Moscovitz. I didn't know what had happened to her, but I assumed Kat was responsible. I fell asleep.

In my dream there was a doll, but it was life-sized, female, made of a thin plastic, had dark hair and eyes, and it lay on Father's operating table. Not young, not old. Father hovered over the prostrate doll, unbuttoned its gingham dress to the waist. Only smooth plastic appeared where her breasts had been. And when he sliced her stomach past her waist, she was missing all of her female organs. Her mouth, ears, shut eyes, nose were all encased in plastic. There was no way in or out of her. Father looked tenderly at the doll, even as he cut off her limbs and began rearranging them.

"There, darling, that looks better," he said to the doll's unchanging face as one arm ended up where a leg used to be, unbending fingers sprouted from her ears, a round buttock protruded from her stomach.

"Wait, let's try this," he said, placing toes on her forehead, sitting the arm from her groin in the space between her anonymous breasts. He moved her internal organs around, draping a stiff stomach across one shoulder, a lung on top of her head, an ear above her heart. He was switching everything around again and again like a puzzle that wasn't completed. He backed away from the doll, which looked freakish with body parts in the wrong places. He studied the photograph pinned near his table. He kissed the doll on what was left of her cheek.

He said, "My darling wife. I keep trying to remember you."

♦　♦　♦　♦　♦

I woke up, lopsided and creased, with too much air choking me.

My tongue whipped around the inside of my mouth, where my teeth had once elbowed one another, forming a fence. A new gap had formed in the back. I spit out two teeth on my pillow. I had lost two molars in my sleep. At least they weren't visible, having emptied from the rear of my mouth. I was losing teeth while I slept! The other parts I had lost from abuse. Now they were simply falling out for no reason. I hid the loose teeth under my pillow because Theresa was crouching on the floor, searching for something. She had opened the window. A rectangular-shaped unending forest, with its congregation of evergreens, and sunlight struggling past the branches, seeped inside the bedroom. It smelled fresh, green, new, and inviting. If only the forest could heal me the way Father's sutures and glue could.

Theresa swung around, the ball and plastic doll wedged under her arm, "Good morning, sleepy Mara. You've slept for two days now. You must be hungry."

"I did?" I was startled. I had never slept that long before, even with all my operations. My time in the world was full of firsts.

"Come on out when you're ready."

"She's finally awake?" the trilling girl's voice said, outside the door.

The little girl, Kat, barged into the room, her hands waving like tentacles. She found her closet door, latched onto that, opening it, rummaging through some noisy objects lodged there, tossing them in a heap onto the floor. Her body shrugged aside broken toys, torn shoes, ripped photographs, shoelaces, plastic bags filled with rocks, shells, brightly colored squares, circles, and triangles.

"You stink like rotten onions." Kat sniffed, "And like an old fire and hunger." Her head was tilted in my general direction. She was clutching a book.

"Conflagration," I whispered to myself.

"What did you say?" the girl asked me loudly.

"What do you need a book for?" I asked the girl, who was pretty accurate with her odors.

"It helps relax her to be read to." Theresa answered. "Come Mara, I have eggs and some bread for you. Then you can take a bath."

"When will she help us, Mama?" The girl's hands began touching every inch of the book as if it could speak to her.

"Soon, Kat, soon." Theresa turned to me. "You can come with me later today on my wash pickup route."

I scooped up my two teeth and stuffed them into my pants pocket. We moved from the child's bedroom into the kitchen where I devoured the meager breakfast. My stomach was delighted with the food, yet was still growling. Theresa began filling up the tub in the bathroom with hot water from the stove. As I sat at the shrunken table I smelled the little girl loitering nearby, fingering her book.

"Today you smell of pine trees, strawberries, dirty fingers," I told the strange girl behind a door. She smiled.

"You're like a dog," she told me.

"Then you're a blind dog," I said. The girl threw her head back and laughed like an adult. Then she ran up to me and fiercely began pummeling me with her tiny fists.

"She hates being reminded that she's blind," Theresa explained, at the sink, her back to us.

I lifted the girl into the air, her fists windmilling, by the collar of her shirt, her uncombed blonde hair thrashing all around her. She was an annoyance. I considered flicking her away. Instead I gently put her down. "I'll read to you when I'm done with my bath."

"Kat, don't be a pest," Theresa said, as she cleaned the dishes. "I'm going to take Mara with me this morning after her bath. Leave her alone."

The girl sighed loudly, her pencil-sized bones shifting into different poses that her mother couldn't see. Some spit worked its way out of the girl's mouth as she muttered to herself. "Good," she managed to say out loud.

The girl appeared fragile but she wasn't. She threw a flimsy fist toward me when she hoped her mother wasn't watching but I caught it and held it. I could have crushed her hand. I stared into her empty eyes that reminded me of unused white paper. "What's it like to have a mother?" I released her hand and she worked it round and round in the air and bit it as though it wasn't a part of her own body.

"Wanting," she said inexplicably.

"Ineffable," I answered her.

♦   ♦   ♦   ♦   ♦

The little girl and I seemed to detect scents that others could not. I found a scrap of paper from a grocery bag and scribbled a quick story before my bath. I could hide it in the blind girl's room.

The Story of Smell

A boy wanted to write about his small, limited life but so far it had smelled fetid. It had the aroma of curdling milk, fungus, old meat. He wanted his life to acquire the odor of freshly baked cookies. One day, at school, he crawled inside a crow. The crow didn't use words. The bird threw his black feathers everywhere but the boy stayed inside the crow. The bird allowed the boy to fly with him to a place crows gathered, making a stinky, white mess.

"Disgusting," the boy yelled, abandoning the crow, filling his nose with black pebbles, breathing out of his mouth, which made it difficult to talk.

"That's the first word of your story," the crow said without talking.

The boy was near a lake and, seeing a black swan, he leaped inside the bird, admiring the bird and feeling safe within its beauty. He sniffed its clean, shimmering feathers, believing he could live inside forever. He would forget about his life story. But as the swan glided from place to place the boy's nose detected all the other animals, which ruined his placid existence. He came out of the swan, smelly and white.

The Solace of Monsters

"I hate these other smells," the boy complained.

The swan turned its lovely black head toward him and told him,
"But it's your scent that is the most disgusting."

Chapter Six

I closed the door to the tiny bathroom and steam somersaulted everywhere, fogging the window, the mirror (my old companion), the toilet, the sink. I rubbed the mirror with my sleeve to see what I looked like to others. My hair was laced with leaves and twigs. My brown eyes were reasonably alert, my eyelashes long and curling. There appeared the mole, the Daughter's mole. I wondered if I could pick it off but it didn't budge. I gave the strange mirror my usual glower. I checked inside my mouth for more damage. I found the space where the two teeth had been.

I cracked a slit in the window and threw my teeth into the woods where I hoped they would grow into tooth trees. I could see tall, thin, white trees with branches studded with teeth instead of leaves or blossoms. I imagined the clacking noise the teeth would make waving in a breeze. I closed the window. I undressed but didn't find any new deletions, just the missing teeth, part of the big toe on my left foot, the other toe, and the top half of my left finger. So far. That might be the end of the subtractions. I wasn't a bad specimen of Mara.

Standing inside the room, I usurped all the space in the bathroom, even hunched over, my head leaning toward my stomach. When I stepped into the hot bath in the tin tub, draping my arms over the sides, there was more space in the room again. I inspected my breasts, the place where others had a belly button but I didn't, my buttocks, my sexual area. I wondered if I could have a child, whether Father had given me working female components on the inside. I doubted it, but it was difficult to know since I'd never used them. I thought that it must be hard to be a mother. Look at Kat.

When I closed my eyes, a memory hugged me, a bassinet with toys dangling above it. A tiny baby wailed in my arms. I rocked the shrieking creature when it wasn't at my breasts, sucking at them eagerly.

"Deirdre," I cooed at the tumultuous, miniature arms and legs, the bald head with its grimacing face. It, too, was new to its body. And it ached for something. Wallpaper with fairytale scenes surrounded us, a fluffy pink rug. With the baby, Deirdre, I was content, although concerned with what she cried for and needed. A warm feeling enveloped me and extended to both of us.

In my memory I closed my eyes, just as I heard footsteps behind me. I put the baby down in her bassinet just before someone's hands clutched at my neck, choking me.

My eyes flicked open just as Kat opened the bathroom door, allowing some of the steam to escape. I stirred the tub water as I reached for my dirty clothes. She was carrying a bundle of new clothes.

"I can't see anything. Remember?" the little girl said, depositing her bundle on the sink. Her hands searched and found my old clothes. "I can hear you splashing."

"Your hair resembles a bird's nest," I told her, sitting back serenely and quietly in the warm water.

She looked surprised. "I'm sure yours doesn't look any better."

"What book are you reading?"

"Goldilocks and the Three Bears."

"I don't know that one."

"One is too small, one is too big, and one is just right," she said loudly as if she was cursing at me.

"Which one is Theresa?" I swirled the tub water to make rippling patterns over my disintegrating body.

"Mama's blind when she wants to be." She looked askance at me with her gluey eyes. "Who are you really?"

"Mara Five," I hesitated, "ish." I was still approximate in this new world.

"Why are you here?"

"That's a long story. Turbulent," I gave her.

"I don't have any friends to tell anyway." She seemed unsatisfied with the word and my answer.

"Neither do I."

"Here are some clean old big men's clothes. Mama said you don't have a mother and that something happened with your father. She said she can tell. Do you have any brothers and sisters?"

I thought for a moment. "Maybe, I don't think so. I don't really know."

She came close to me, whispered, "I have an older brother. But we haven't seen him since our father died. Peter. Sometimes I can hear him in the woods." She laughed strangely, as though water was being poured over her, and left.

♦ ♦ ♦ ♦ ♦

I was wearing the shapeless shirt and thick, baggy pants Theresa had given me, warm, clean socks, my old shoes. I was taller than most people so a slice of my waist peeked out from the shirt. We would wash my old clothes as soon as we picked up the rest of the laundry from the people who would pay us. Theresa noticed my missing toes when I put the socks on in the kitchen.

"Were you in an accident?"

"No. Actually yes, several." Just the accident of Father creating me and my body turning against me.

"I see you've lost some of your finger."

"Yes, fairly recently."

Theresa came over to where I was sitting, patted me on the

back. "Don't worry, you're safe here. No one will find you out here, in the forest. People can disappear out here for years. My husband used to go hunting for days. And my son, Peter, might still be out there somewhere. He came home the day after they found my husband, and left, and I haven't heard from him since. I miss him. He must be somewhere."

The little girl wandered into the room. She bumped into the wash tub filled with soapy water in the middle of the floor.

"Sorry, Kat," her mother said, "I moved it. I'm just getting ready to do the wash this afternoon. I should have warned you."

The girl grabbed a spoon, with the oval center cut out, from the counter. She felt for the hole, dipped it into the soapy water and began blowing bubbles, which flew into the air like a flock of round, transparent birds. I had never seen anything so elegant and beautiful. Clear yet full of rainbow colors. The bubbles shimmered and twisted, dipped and rose, crashed into one another, burst, fell back into soap puddles. They lived their whole life cycles within a few seconds. Born, flew, and returned to their origins.

Theresa was wiping up what remained of the burst bubbles splattered on the floor. "It's too bad you can't see the bubbles, Kat."

"I can feel them." The little girl pinched one as it inflated from her spoon while she blew on it. It collapsed, became wet water again all over her hands. "I can see them inside me." Kat's head shifted. "Mara?"

"Yes."

"I want to feel your face."

I didn't want her to, but I extended my head toward her, remembering some of the operations. "Here," I offered.

Her hands nibbled my face, patting, caressing, twitching, halting at a scar site, then at the mole. "Having a mother is like seeing colors," the little girl whispered into my convoluted ear. Her active hands finally stopped wandering. "Yes," she said, "you are large and you shouldn't be afraid of anything."

"Life isn't always so simple, Kat," her mother instructed her. "Okay, Mara, let's go." Theresa was carrying several empty sacks.

Everything smelled fresh and clean, including me. Even the little girl's hair looked brushed and the dazzling color of sunlight. It amazed me how much of a person's history could be washed away.

♦ ♦ ♦ ♦ ♦

I hadn't really noticed the woods before. They had surrounded Father's house like an inadvertent gate. They crept toward Theresa's house as though they were trying to surprise her or consume the house and yard.

"Subterfuge," I murmured to myself.

I reminisced about running through the forest a few days ago, but I hadn't really experienced the woods. Only at night and only as a difficult, threatening geography to leave behind. In truth the forest was a companion.

"Gloves," I whispered to myself.

Bathed and with some food and sleep, the woods insisted on offering me pines, spruce, Douglas fir, elm, junipers. I could hear a river between the leaves, cotoneaster shrubs, sagebrush, thickets. I'd read a botany book at Father's but I didn't know how a plant felt or smelled as they pushed their way into the world. There were crags and mountains in the distance that thrust their faces into the sky, as if the sky, too, was blind and trying to visualize them by touching them. The profusion of every green thing kept on tapping my shoulders and head, brushing my back and legs. The world was incredibly beautiful when I wasn't running through it. Butterflies, moths, and iridescent flies filled space not strangled with vines or trees. Birds chattered their boisterous songs and called to one another.

Theresa hesitated a moment, crushed the leaves of a common tansy bush, held it beneath my nostrils, allowed the odor of camphor and menthol to fill my nose, reminding me of Father's laboratory. For one second I could hear the clatter of metal instruments, the whirring and thumping of machines, bright lights focused on me and bounced away, something thick and wet being cut open, and then that brief memory faded.

I could detect the hidden scratching of rodents and rabbits, fox, the clandestine movements of deer. The forest was so alive in a way I hadn't seen from my window. It was full of movement, smell, taste, small noises. Blossoms had fallen and seeds and pods had dispersed, swarming and lying fallow and waiting on the ground for the ideal circumstances to grow and thrive. Purple lupines, red poppies, asters, paintbrush, lichen, mushrooms stood at attention, wanting to be noticed. I wanted to call to Theresa, up ahead, to stop walking while I stood still and became a part of the forest like some large, ravaged tree. I wanted to sit, listen, smell, become a part of what had been growing all around me all those years and I hadn't been able to touch it.

Finally Theresa sat down on a huge, jutting rock that she said could have once been part of a glacier. "How are we going to explain you to the people I work for?"

"Ubiquitous," I threw at her, having no idea how these things worked, politeness and explanations.

"You're a strange one sometimes, Mara. I don't know what you're talking about half the time." Her brows drew together, her skin rippling like water. I noticed a small thin scar near her hairline. "I can't say that you're a family member like some long-lost cousin because I grew up here and everybody knows my family and my business." Her features drew together contemplatively. "How about saying that you're a friend of Peter's he met in another town and you're visiting for a while? You can say you didn't know that he wasn't living here anymore when you stopped by."

"That's when a person says one thing but means another, lying. It's complicated," I said. I thought of Father and how he had described the world.

"I hate to ask you to lie, but if we don't, whoever is looking for you will find you, and all my customers will be suspicious of an outsider." Theresa shook her head. "That's just the way this town is."

"Father told me that the world is difficult and full of wars, crime, famine, rapes, and shootings."

"Outside here, yes." She nodded. "We have our own problems, but we don't have big city problems here. At least not yet. Or not in the way you might think."

"I don't really understand the ways of the world."

"That's okay, Mara. Your father must have kept you isolated, which isn't a bad thing raising a kid." She patted my knee. "I can use you, and work will keep you busy and your mind off of terrible things. And church helps." She lifted my chin with her hand. "I'll explain things to you the best I can."

I nodded, and her hand dropped away. "I still haven't met God yet." I was thinking about the church.

Theresa roared with laughter. "I can't say many of us have."

"I thought that was why people went to church."

Theresa laughed again but didn't say anything.

I pointed at her forehead. "I see that you have a scar too."

"It's old." Theresa rose from the rock, retied her shoes. "We're almost to the first house. Mr. John Benjamin, he's an old-timer. He was born here, grew up here, and he'll die here. He never married and I've been doing his laundry for years. So you know what to say, Mara, if anyone asks you?"

I nodded. I didn't like lying, but I could see it had its advantages.

We were walking again. A cluster of buildings appeared with sidewalks and a dirt road down the center. The town was dug out of the forest. The houses seemed old, peeling, leaning toward the ground like scraggly weeds. I could ascertain a bar, a grocery, a clothes shop, and a post office. Was it a mirage, flickering in sunlight since the trees had been cleared around the space? A few cars gathered there, and I thought I could see someone pacing and smoking outside the bar. We veered away from the town and went down a side road, arriving at a house that seemed to have a lopsided smile and was covered with tumbleweeds. A smallish dog, chained to a piece of old farm equipment, barked repeatedly at us. I could smell its disturbance, cigar smoke, burnt onions and eggs. Black and white colors leaped toward me. It ran to the end of its chain, choked itself as it tried to snap at us.

"Obstreperous," I offered Theresa. I felt sorry for the dog.

"Calvin, be quiet," Theresa told the dog. It whimpered and followed its tail until it sat down in the dirt.

When we approached the house, the front door flew open and an ancient man stepped out onto the dilapidated porch. He was the oldest man I had ever seen. His organs and limbs would be useless for Father's experiments. He smiled broadly and his face was wrinkled beyond recognition.

"Mr. John Benjamin, this here's Mara, a friend of Peter's who stopped by to see us, but she didn't know he was gone. Mara, this is Mr. Benjamin and you'll be picking up his laundry from now on."

At least I didn't have to lie. The old man picked at his teeth with a miniature piece of wood and spit at the ground. "You can call me John." He turned to Theresa, "She's a strong-looking one."

"Yes, she is," Theresa continued, "I might have her doing the cleaning soon too. First we'll see how the regular washing goes. That's you and Miss Elaina for now."

"I keep on threatening Theresa that someday I'll get a washer and dryer." The old man gargled his laughter. Theresa had a light, wispy laugh. Then there was my terrible grinding guffaw. They were both startled by it.

"You sound like a broken lawn mower." Then the man laughed again. "Do you girls want any coffee before you go?"

"No, but thanks for the offer." Theresa picked up a large dirty brown bag on his slanting porch and slung it over her shoulders. She handed it to me when she came down the rotten steps.

The dog's barking began again. It was straining at its chain.

I put the laundry bag down and ripped the chain off of the old thrasher so the dog was free. I dragged the dog, which pulled away, toward me and lifted it up by its collar. I held it still in my hands as I raised them over my head. I didn't care whether I unintentionally crushed the noisy, unhappy dog or not. It needed to learn about limits and freedom, a lecture Father often gave me. Its turbulence was the owner's fault, not the dog's. I opened my palms and Calvin, the dog, frantically twirled around on them. The dog barked and circled but had nowhere to go, and it wouldn't jump from that height. Finally the dog calmed down after kicking its legs and smelling and nibbling at my hands. The only other choice was to let the dog free, into the forest, where it could be injured. And, like me, the dog would have its day.

When it sat quietly, I said, "Good dog, Calvin." I let it loose on the ground, and it barked once at me and then ran to the old man. It lay down on the porch, the collar and a small piece of chain resting along its back.

"There," I said, "now the dog's free. It doesn't need the chain and it will remember me and be good next time I come." I picked up the man's bag of laundry and hoisted it onto my back.

"I hope so," the old man said, shaking his head.

When we had walked far enough away from the house, Theresa exclaimed, "I sure hope you know what you're doing."

"I must figure it out as I go along." I didn't know why I did what I did, but I received a brief memory of dancing with a man in a tuxedo, a band played behind us, and other couples in long gowns danced slowly around us. I twirled on my own in the center of a dance floor, and a large dog ran out from an inner room, stopped at the hem of my dress, lunged at my leg and bit me. I was perplexed, then bleeding.

"I don't want to lose any customers." She wagged a finger at me. "The next one is a retired schoolteacher, and she's probably seen everything. She was my teacher when I was a child." Theresa trudged ahead.

We passed glimpses through thin trees of the town, which consisted of three neon signs, several large windows full of merchandise, a radio blared through the two long streets, from one end to the other. A few people entered or exited cars. Everything seemed old, as if the town, as well as the people, were living in a past time. A ghost town I had seen in a book. Father, too, wanted to live or relive another time from his life, and I wondered if all humans, because of memories, were fated to cherish either the past or the future, ignoring the present.

The next house was closer to town and had a much neater appearance, like that of a freshly baked cake. It had been painted recently, was upright, and the plants and grass around it were tidy. No dogs barked as we approached the front door, which had a bell. Theresa repeated her rehearsed lie about me when a woman older than Theresa opened the door. She had white hair in a bun, thick eyeglasses, and her eyes, like fish underwater, swam toward me and remained on my face as though I had smeared breakfast on my nose unknowingly. At her doorstep I inhaled deeply, catching the odor of books, filled with stale paper, orange juice, and something fruity and light, perfume I think, which I had never smelled before. Theresa and the woman were exchanging pleasantries. I closed my eyes, but a memory of being on a plane that was falling out of the sky began to overtake me, so I opened them quickly. My stomach lurched back into place. I scratched my ear and the curved top rim, the helix with a bit of the triangular fossa, bloodlessly fell into my hand. I slipped it into my pants pocket, patted the hair covering my ear. Memories began arriving faster than they had previously. I was trying to direct them more, on and off like the computer.

"Are you unwell?" Miss Elaina's glasses were focused on me.

"Except for losing things from my body I don't want to lose I am perfectly fine." Then I realized that I had answered too honestly. They were both staring at me.

"Come inside and sit a while, both of you." Miss Elaina swept us inside with a gesture of her hand. Theresa told me to leave the old man's laundry bag at the doorstep. I ducked into the house, which was roomier than Theresa's.

We were seated on an embroidered sofa. Every surface and piece of furniture in her living room had curlicues or stitched finery. Everything was embellished and feminine. I had only seen rooms like hers in magazines. It was full of small objects that had no purpose except for a collection, decoration, or to remind Miss Elaina of another time. Porcelain cats, thimbles from various states, doilies, a pink hurricane lamp. Theresa's home wasn't like this one. Everything here was delicate or breakable. I needed to be cautious in my movements.

"Exactly what things?" Miss Elaina inspected me with her eyes. "You do have several scars." She lifted my limp wrists. I pulled them back toward my body.

"I've told her that she can explain everything to me when she's ready," Theresa stated.

"Do you have books and writing implements here?" I was excited by the implications.

"Of course I do. I was a teacher here. Would you like some tea?" she addressed us both.

"Yes, please."

Miss Elaina sat in a carved wooden chair with a straight back but I still towered over her, even sitting, which made me feel clumsier than usual in her dainty house. I would practice all the etiquette I had learned from Father and Theresa. Miss Elaina left the room.

"I need to get back to Kat. I don't like her wandering alone in the woods so much," Theresa whispered to me. "So I can't stay here. If you want to remain, can you find your way back to the house?"

"Yes, and I can carry both bags of washing back home for you."

"Are you sure you can do that? It gets pretty heavy. I had a cart for a while, but it got caught in the bushes and on rocks and stuff so I stopped using it."

I stood up, walked behind the sofa, with Theresa still sitting on it, I bent down, gripped the sofa from underneath and lifted it a foot or so into the air. Theresa gasped. I gently dropped the couch back into its rightful place and sat back down on it.

"Why do you worry about Kat? She seems capable of taking care of herself."

"I know she can be trying, and she hates everyone, but I'm her mother."

"Misanthropic," I gave Theresa. Like Father. Theresa didn't seem to care about the gift of words. "What do you do as her mother?"

"It's my job to protect her and to love her."

"Love can annihilate, or destroy," I explained.

"Some kinds of love. You're different, Mara, strong though. That's a good thing. I don't need to worry about you. Just be polite to Miss Elaina. Anyway, you can come to church with me on Sunday. There's another kind of love there." She rose and called out to the kitchen, "Miss Elaina, I'm sorry, I have to go and take care of Kat, but Mara will stay for a little while." She left before I could ask her any more questions.

Miss Elaina returned carrying a tray with gold cups and saucers and a steaming teapot, which she placed on the table in front of me. Peppermint coiled in the air, then rested on our shoulders. It was light and green. A small cross with the sad, dying man hung on her wall.

"Have you met God at the church?"

Miss Elaina giggled, like glass splintering. "God's probably the last person you'd meet there." She poured the peppermint tea so the odor spread toward the edges of the room and rested there. She lifted a cup to her lips. "You do know that you can meet God anywhere, don't you?"

I was shocked. "No, no one told me that. How?"

"I can't tell you. I haven't seen Him. Except for glimpsing Him through a few incredible people I've met." She sipped. "Seeing Him never lasted for me. I must admit I've given up on Him."

My mouth gaped. "Are you a mother?"

"You certainly are a direct young woman." She peered at me, her eyeglasses fogging as she sipped her tea. "No, I don't have any children of my own, and I've never been married. So who am I to teach others? What about you?"

"I don't think I can have children. I've met only one available man so far and it didn't end well."

"Was there anything else you wanted to know before you take the laundry?"

"There is so much I have to learn," I mumbled to myself. "Can I see your books?"

She appeared startled by our conversation. She placed the tea cup on the table. "Certainly, come." She showed me to another room in the house that had bookshelves from the floor to the tall ceiling. There was a table and two chairs by a window.

I gasped. It was my turn to be startled. "Is this a library?"

"This is MY library." She touched a few of the books. "But you're right. This is bigger than the library behind the post office."

"Can I borrow some books?" I twirled round and round. "I don't know where to begin."

"Perhaps when I know you better I can make some suggestions. I want to make sure you'll take good care of my books."

"I have so much to learn. My father allowed me only certain books."

"What did you want to learn about first?" Miss Elaina's fingers brushed one of her books.

"How to filter through memories," I said, haltingly. "No, the relationship between parents and children. Or all about God." I looked at Miss Elaina inquiringly. "I don't know how to choose. I don't know anything."

She slammed her book shut. "That's it. I'll find you a book all about life, full of life, for next time." She walked out of the room. "We can discuss it, too, if you want."

"Can I have a pen and a notebook?"

"For what?"

"I want to write down my stories and adventures."

"Don't we all, Mara. But I suppose Theresa doesn't have much in the way of pen and paper."

I shook my head.

She rummaged through some boxes in another room. "Here," she said, tearing out some pages in a miniature book with a black and white splattered cardboard cover. The name Sandy Shane was scribbled on a blank line on the front with some crude pictures. She handed me a few pens. "For now you need to go." She pointed toward her pink tiled bathroom. "And there's my washing." She opened her front door.

"Audacious," I gave her as I was leaving.

"Yes you are," she said from her doorstep.

She was the only other person, besides Father, who understood the value of words.

Chapter Seven

On the way home that afternoon, as I walked through the woods, I relished the various shades of green, the touches of yellow or red on leaves and flowers, the brown of logs or tree trunks. Under my feet the smell of crushed greenery, fresh and growing, lifted toward my nostrils. Weeds, long grass, and ferns tickled my pant legs and shoes. Sunlight jeweled the trees, made patterns on the bark. I enjoyed the way evergreens hoisted up the sky, opening into all that blue. I detected the scent of cows, their digestions and excrement, the slow way they scraped against and shifted within their fences. I smelled horses, and thought of the way they penetrated everything with their hooves, tearing up the landscape as they ran through it. Those horses, with their large, expressive eyes, swished at flies with their lovely manes and tails. How they could run in all different directions at the same time. I liked all the animals, all the plants, maybe even better than people.

I neared Theresa's house. My load did not feel very heavy. But I put it down near a small rock. I heard the uncomfortable squealing of a mouse, claws digging at dirt. I didn't understand the sound. A spider surprised me by swinging near my face, then alighting again on its thinly woven web. I missed the companionship of mice. I grew closer to the noise and spied Kat sitting on the ground pulling something elastic and gray in her hands. Then she threw it against a tree. I saw a tail.

"Ouch," she cried and began sucking on her fingers.

A twig crackled under my feet and her head with its boisterous hair snapped upward, in my direction.

"Who's there? Peter? Who's watching me?" She scowled in my direction.

"It's me, Mara." I emerged from my hiding place. "What are you doing there? Didn't your mother find you?"

"I'm playing and my mother knows I'm out here." She grimaced, her hand reaching toward the unmoving gray mass.

I moved closer, saw the dead mouse. "What did you do to it?" My voice was growing louder and louder.

"It bit me. I made it fly away."

"You're a monster," I screamed at her. She did it on purpose. "Do you think you're a god?" I yelled.

"Animals and people die too easily," she said, touching what was left of the companion mouse's body. "I don't know where they go. They just don't move anymore."

"You've done this before?" Was she different than Father even though she was a child?

She didn't answer me. "You're the monster," she yelled back at me as she rose, seemed sure of her way back to the house. She didn't need to use her hands much. "And we don't want you here."

I sat on a rotting log. Ants crawled near me with their frantic processions. I aligned my bones, tried to feel normal. I breathed steadily. Light penetrated the trees in pieces, arrived at my feet in various shapes. I wondered if I gathered all the pieces together whether I, too, could create another creature, a creature made entirely of light. At least no one would be hurt by that.

I removed the top part of my ear from my pants pocket. That missing part was covered by my hair and couldn't be seen. I threw it toward the small clearing where Kat had been sitting. A gray squirrel leaped near, its tail bristling and full. It dug around my prostrate ear top, sat on its haunches, lifted and twirled my curved ear piece between its paws, as another squirrel arrived to watch it. Then the squirrel put my ear in its mouth and leaped away. I began to think about trees that grew ears or fingers or toes, an innocuous method for Father to find the parts for me that he needed. He could simply pick one from the correct type of tree during flowering season. There could be trees growing internal organs too, heart conifers, liver oaks, vascular maples, kidney ash, lung spruce, pancreatic pine.

I sighed. Kat was correct; I was a monster too. I couldn't help it though. Kat could. I closed my eyes and received another memory that I didn't try to stop.

I was painting on a large canvas. Different colors were splashed onto the white, and I tried to match my brushstrokes with my mood, which was mixed, inspired, despairing, and hopeful. A face emerged from the maelstrom of color as I used black on my palette knife. Done, I stepped back.

"Interesting," my husband said. He rubbed his chin, "The forest with that small, gray animal emerging. What were you trying to do?"

"A self-portrait."

I opened my eyes and thought I saw someone watching me from behind some bushes. I stomped over there, past where Kat had sat, and parted the leaves and branches, but no one was there. I wasn't sure Kat could move that quickly.

I smiled. I'd received a memory that wasn't an incredible, emotive moment of extinguishment. It had been a moment of self-realization, a memory that could teach me something. I could learn to live more fully through these memories, to make them my own. Was this one trying to tell me about my own creation? How a painter creates themselves over and over again? And how do I see myself?

"Cohesive," I whispered to myself. With every step I was losing and gaining.

I rose and noticed something flesh-colored under a fern. When I parted the fronds I found Miss Moscovitz, her head twisted aside with its explosion of blonde hair. She was lying on some moss. Her body was riddled with scars, deep gouges, and sprawled near some fallen tree limbs. Had Kat thrown her against a tree by mistake? Or worse, had Kat inflicted these injuries on purpose? Was this how she treated what she cared about? I understood the doll.

I pulled out the notebook Miss Elaina had given me. Where Sandy Shane had written her name, I crossed it out, put *Mara F.* I was evolving. I opened the cardboard cover, wrote *Exegesis* on the top of the first page, my interpretation of Father's work. We, all the Maras, were alive. I penned *Maybe the memories were real and Father, Theresa, Kat, and this very green world were a dream.* I had so many impulses in this world outside of Father's laboratory and house. But I didn't know which of them were important. Instead of my adventures, maybe I could use the notebook as a journal.

I rose and gathered what was left of Miss Moscovitz in the two laundry bags, stuffing my small notebook inside one of them. A late afternoon mist on the ground ghosted my ankles. A wind began, and leaves whispered in an uncomfortable manner. I peered back into the deeper forest and I glimpsed a running tuft of blonde hair. I wasn't sure what held me together.

◆　◆　◆　◆　◆

At the house Theresa had begun making dinner and Kat was blowing those beautiful bubbles from the washing tin. I deposited the laundry bags near Kat's legs.

"Kat brought me Solomon's Seal to make tea and huckleberries that I'm cooking with venison, all from the woods." Theresa beamed, looking briefly at Kat, "She does well out in these woods. She even brought wildflowers." A mass of bent flowers poked in every direction from a glass on the eating table.

"Are there any computers or phones nearby?" I asked, curious and unsure what could be discovered.

Theresa thought for a moment. "Someone in town, maybe a merchant, might have a computer in a back room. Everyone in town has a phone, but we don't get much reception outside of town. Who would we call out here? Besides, Kat and I don't have the money. Did you need to contact someone?"

"No, I was just asking." I could see how one life fell open into another one. "I found this along my way," I held out the doll to Kat. Then I realized and lifted her arm, and I placed the head and torso into her small hand. "Miss Moscovitz had been ravaged on the path home."

Theresa looked at me sadly, then at Kat.

Kat tossed her aside. Her body skidded and came to rest at Theresa's feet and her head rolled into a corner. "I don't want her anymore."

"Why? What's the matter, Kat? What happened?" Theresa asked, with concern in her voice.

"Nothing. Miss Moscovitz was trying to climb a tree and she fell down and her head came off."

Theresa picked up the doll parts. She tried to put them back together. "You could still play with her."

"I don't want her anymore. I said already." She was glowering.

I knew how Miss Moscovitz felt, although Father still wanted me back. He just didn't want the real me.

"But Kat, we don't have any money for a new doll."

"I don't care." She turned away from her mother with her vacant eyes.

"Maybe I can ask in town and see if anyone has any old dolls for you." Theresa, with her dark hair knotted in a flowered scarf, moved toward us like an impending horizon. She carried plates of food. The aroma filled me. But, as she grew closer, I became hungrier, my stomach groaned, being absolutely precise in its need. Theresa made the three of us plates of food, but Kat moved her fingers onto Theresa's plate and scooped food into her mouth with her hands.

When she tried to taste mine, I chided her, "You know who the plates belong to."

"I want yours."

"You have your own," I told her, and she didn't come near my food again.

The little girl grunted as an acknowledgement. She was eating her own food aggressively.

"Tonight, Kat, you can sleep in your room again. You'll have to share it with Mara. So be a good girl, please." Theresa ate what was left of her dinner, daintily with a knife and fork.

"Avaricious," I explained. But neither of them understood. "And garrulous," I continued. The little girl crawled underneath my skin. She was trying to mark her territory. I continued, "I understand the need for money to eat and for things, but I don't understand why people want more than what's necessary."

Kat snickered.

"To get ahead, Mara. So people can fulfill their dreams." Theresa tapped Kat's shoulder.

"I dreamt about a road lined with angels once," I explained.

"Not night dreams. I mean things you hope for during the day like fixing up our church, being able to buy Kat toys, visiting somewhere, or going to the doctor if someone gets sick. Things like that."

But I didn't completely understand it. Father complained about his job sometimes but it was how he made money to create the Maras in his basement. That was his dream. I did miss him. The old Father before me and the Maras, that was never discussed. That father must have had different dreams. I didn't always see what Father called The Big Picture.

"Father always claimed that the body was temperamental. Like a fussy clock. One small component could go out of whack and destroy something. He said the different parts were reliant on one another. People could continue with only one kidney, but not without a heart or liver or stomach. We could persevere with one arm or leg but not without one head." I had given them one of Father's lectures. I glanced at the little girl. "Kat seems to do fine with her blindness." She was missing one of her senses.

"Someday I'd like a doctor, a specialist, to take another look." Theresa tossed a look at Kat that she couldn't see.

"Mama, I do okay." Kat grabbed a red crayon from a pile.

We were finished eating and Theresa was cleaning up the dishes. "Your father sounds like an interesting man. Is he a doctor or something?" she asked.

"Or something. I don't know. I think he once was a doctor but he does research now."

"What kind?'

"I don't know."

"Mara, come over here," Kat yelled loudly.

I did.

"Mara needs to help me with the laundry. What do you need, Kat?"

"Lie down on the floor."

I did. Kat gleefully traced my outline in red crayon on the floor.

"You're so big. You could wrestle wolves and bears."

"I'm an archetype, one-of-a-kind."

"Please don't make a mess, Kat," Theresa screamed from the kitchen.

"You shouldn't be afraid of anything," the frightening little girl said.

"Some days I'm afraid of everything," I confessed.

"That's silly. You could live in the forest like Peter and have plenty to eat."

"I don't know how."

"Kat, Peter's gone. He doesn't live in the forest," Theresa added.

The little girl bent down to my ear and whispered, "She doesn't know anything."

"What would Peter be doing in the forest?" Theresa asked.

"Living," the creepy girl answered.

"Why wouldn't he come home?"

Kat didn't say anything.

I rose and began doing the laundry. Theresa directed me while she finished up the dishes. Kat went outside to play.

"Not too late tonight and I'll call you when it gets dark," Theresa told her.

"Next week, on Tuesday," Theresa hovered over the washing tub, "we'll be going to the big city to see some cousins. Mack in town has to drive in and pick up some stuff for his store and we can go along with him. Would you like to come, Mara?"

"Are all the other forests like this one?"

"They are similar, maybe with different species of trees and animals and with different weather. Have you been to a city before, Mara?"

"I haven't seen much of the world." I gave myself, "Palpable."

◆　◆　◆　◆　◆

I read *Goldilocks and the Three Bears* to Kat in our bedroom after she told me that she wanted me out of her room very soon or else Peter would come in the middle of the night and throw me out. She lay on her small bed with her legs crossed. I was on my bed on the floor. There wasn't any space left in the room.

"I don't even believe he exists. Like Goldilocks, who is a fictional character," I explained to the little girl.

"He does," she screamed. "He knows how to hide, how to live in the woods since our father taught him."

"Why would he do that when he has a home here?" But I knew there were many different reasons to escape.

"You're Goldilocks," the girl was screaming again. Her hair was dirty and crept around her neck like a vine. "You eat our porridge, sit in our chairs, sleep in my room. They are all too small for you. You came out of the forest, and you'll go away and never come back to the home of the three bears." She smiled triumphantly.

"First of all, you are two bears. . . ," I began logically.

"Peter too."

"And I'm more like the big bear than Goldilocks."

"It's just a story." She stuck out her tongue, then banged her fists against the wall.

"Would you eat me like the bears if I was Goldilocks?"

"In a minute." She snapped her tiny teeth. "Goldilocks was scared after taking everything."

"What if none of the three bears was perfect? One was too small, one too big, and one still wasn't right?"

The girl didn't answer me. She lay on her bed in her disheveled pajamas decorated with faded elephants. We could hear damp laundry flapping on the numerous clotheslines that Theresa's husband had built for her business. The rows reached back into the woods like long, thin roads. The sound was eerie and constant in a breeze, like muffled footsteps. At least they didn't grow any closer.

"Do you miss your father?" I asked the little girl who reclined on her back with her eyes closed.

"He hit Mama," the girl barely whispered as she was exhaling. She sighed, turned onto her side, facing the wall.

"Reprehensible," I gave her since I didn't have anything else to offer her. But she, the Childcloud, was already asleep and breathing steadily.

I wrote in my notebook: *I didn't really understand my father. There is so much I still don't understand. All the books have helped me with the world, but there are subtleties I can't grasp.*

There is both good and evil in a little girl.

Everything is about the body.

The moon was trying to thrust itself past our curtains. Its light reminded me of muscles under the skin of this house, a motion. Movement was spreading, opening one door and then another.

I tried to imagine the city, tall buildings stacked onto one another. All those people and cars threading, held onto the ground by questionable gravity. There were so many activities and colors, noises, tastes, and odors were torrential. Everyone leaked onto everyone else. People lived in compartments. Some people were withering, some were thriving like weeds. All who disappeared there were reappearing.

It grew quiet. "Taciturn," I exhaled.

I fell asleep.

◆　◆　◆　◆　◆

My dream was of a city full of creatures like me, sewn, glued, stitched together from other parts, enormous, strong, larger-than-life. Cats like Gloves roamed cement streets and alleyways searching for mice who were also pieced together and losing their tails, ears, paws, sometimes a nose or an eye. A ramshackle man swept the streets and roads with a large broom, tossing lost animal and human body parts into his garbage.

As I walked down a street I greeted Childclouds who were new and fresh to life. White birds seemed to fly out of their mouths from their recent operations. The Childclouds held the scarred hands of a Mara that didn't look like me and a male creature unlike anyone I had seen before. I didn't recognize them, except one that resembled Carl, who had driven the car, and one old man, who was an older version of Father. They filled the streets. I stopped to peer in the window of a restaurant and saw an older waitress, with a likeness to Miss Elaina, whose hand flew off onto the floor when she tried to pick up a customer's emptied plate of food. The waitress laughed, and so did her customers, and then she stooped and picked it up, subsequently dropping it into her apron pocket. I overheard her say to an adolescent creature, "I'll just have to get another one."

As I continued down the street I noticed that buildings, doors, windows, steps, cars, and buses were all bigger to accommodate us. The people I saw often reminded me of people from my memories that weren't really mine. I didn't know if there was a city full of Fathers who created these new fully grown Childclouds or just one working furiously, maybe with assistants, to fill the city. All of us one-of-a-kinds, with our own cars, jobs, storefronts selling clothes (with removable sleeves or pant legs in case some part wore out). I passed a shop with an auto mechanic underneath a car, who had no legs and he was scooting everywhere on a skateboard. He smiled at me with a lopsided grin webbed with scars. Were we all disintegrating? Then replenished?

A dog bounded up to me who was on a leash. "Berserk," I cried. She leaped onto my legs. We greeted and kissed each other. I noticed that she had a different tail and a patch of black fur near a hind leg that was different from her brown and white, long, silky fur. Her owner reminded me of Greg. I had to turn away from him.

"Sorry," I exclaimed, "a misperception."

"Malingerer," he threw at me as he pulled the dog to leave.

◆ ◆ ◆ ◆ ◆

I woke suddenly. The little girl had Miss Moscovitz and was removing her tattered clothes. The doll's head was wobbly but attached to her body again. What was left of the hair was smoother and thinner. It was an updated doll. Theresa must have fixed her in the night.

"What are you doing, Kat?" I asked her, sitting up from the floor.

"Nothing." She whisked the doll behind her. "Playing." She fidgeted.

There was a knock at the door and Theresa poked her head inside. "Today is church, so you girls get yourself ready." Then she closed the door behind her.

The little girl grimaced, made her way, surefooted, to her closet. With her hands outstretched she found a dress trellised with flowers and edged with lace. "I hate dresses."

"Why must you wear one to church when God is everywhere?"

"I don't know. Ask my mother." She turned her blind eyes toward me, "We have to take baths first. I hate those too."

"Does your mother want you to look like someone she is thinking of?" I fingered my mole.

"I guess so. Or else it's because everybody from town is in church." Kat made a funny face, twisting her features around purposefully.

"Did your father ever hurt you?"

"No, but he hurt Peter." She faced the wall.

The forest couldn't help peering in our window. Light rushed into our room, grew giddy around all the furniture and toys. A bird skittered from branch to branch and flew past our window. I touched the glass. Flowers gathered around stones and vegetation. The wash on the clotheslines was stiff under the blue sky, but became boisterous with the tumultuous clouds.

"Do you want me to describe the morning to you, Kat? There's so much going on. It's beautiful." I knew I could open the window, walk out the door, and hardly look back. Was I feral?

"I don't want to know about stuff I can't see," she said dejectedly.

"We all long for what we can't see or have yet." It was something Father could have said.

105

Chapter Eight

The church was filled with people wearing their fanciest clothes. When I usually saw it, it was empty except for Theresa and me. Women wore hats punctuated with feathers, ribbons, or bows, and pale dresses choked with flowers or lace, attractive hems and seams twitching around their torsos. The men were dressed in dark, stiff suits as if they needed to prepare for a death. Many of the outfits were familiar to us because Theresa and I had washed them recently. Theresa had returned the laundry, but it would be my job this week. Theresa, Kat, and I wore our most resplendent dresses. Theresa had patched together several dresses that she had found in unclaimed laundry piles from women who had died or moved away to make my dress, which hardly fit me. I didn't have a hat.

"Ostentatious," I told myself quietly. "Church is so unscientific," I complained to Theresa. "And I still haven't found God." I looked around. Theresa was sitting complacently on the pew next to me. Kat sat squirming next to her.

"It's hard for the living to understand higher beings," Theresa said softly.

"You mean the dead?" I inquired, immediately interested.

"Those who have already completed their lives or . . . like when an animal is about to give birth, those that dwell in the place the newly born come from."

I knew partly where I came from. I'd seen Greg's body. I had memories that informed me. But I had no idea where I was going. "Does church tell us where we go?"

"Sort of," Theresa explained, "but, as you said, it's not scientific."

"Shh," said an older woman whose white head immediately drooped close to her lap.

"Flummoxed," I gave myself, enjoying the entertaining word.

I didn't spy Miss Elaina, but I located Mr. John Benjamin in a suit that reminded me of me since it appeared to be unthreading and had patches at his elbows and knees. He waved, a floppy black book precarious in his hands.

A young, rough-looking, unknown man with black hair sidled close to Theresa and the little girl, said, "Hello, Kat, sweetheart." She grabbed her mother's arm. Then he spoke over their heads to me, "I couldn't help noticing this lovely woman here. What's your name, darling?"

I smelled cigarettes, liquor, sweat, and something like bean soup permeating his skin. I turned away. "Mara." I stood, my size overshadowing him.

"Mara, you can't put one over on me. I'll catch you later." He pointed his finger at me and wagged it, tilted his smirking face.

"That's Fred. Stay away from him, Mara. I don't like him near Kat either," Theresa warned.

I didn't have time to ask her why because a man in black and white, the minister, began orating from the podium. The wooden cross with that sad, injured man was suspended behind him. I received a memory while the minister was speaking, men rolling up a large scroll, men bowing and praying under shawls near black books collapsed into rows. I was sitting in a balcony with women. They were speaking a language I didn't understand, but I nodded. I was thinking about building a golem out of straw, mud, and stone. Why would I need such a creature? Did the golem resemble me, except that it was male? When the memory disappeared, I wanted to cry, thinking how fragile human beings really were.

Singing filled my ears, my skeleton vibrated, my elaborate circuitry tuned in to each note yet absorbed the melody, the rhythm. My tongue wished to surge, catch every phrase and repeat it. My pulse jumped, and I froze at the music's fluidity. My remaining toes were tapping. The music smelled of vanilla, sugar, baked eggs, caramel.

"You must not have heard much music before," Theresa laughed after the service, "because we're not that good here, being a little church and all."

When I bit into a chocolate chip cookie, I lost another tooth, this time halfway between the front and back of my mouth. I spit it into a napkin and threw it away. *Entropy* I would write in my journal to explain. People were eddying in groups. Several couples complimented Theresa on the upkeep of the church.

"Mara is helping so much," she told them.

"It's good to have a purpose in life," a wife told me and Theresa.

"What's my purpose?" I asked Theresa. I thought that my purpose was one thing with Father, another to companion animals, and another thing here with Theresa. Maybe I was composed of many purposes.

"You have to figure it out yourself. I'm a mother and I was a wife," Theresa stated, sipping some coffee.

Kat knocked over some hot coffee cups with her roving hands. She was bumping into people's legs, blinking her blind eyes. She parked herself in a corner of the hewn wood church, and she began dancing in circles to some unheard music. She crawled on the floor and then raced her fingers up a wall.

Theresa spotted her antics. "Kat's bored. Maybe you could walk her home, Mara. I'll be there soon. This is the only chance I get to talk to certain people all week."

"Raucous," I stated. I walked over to the little girl. "Come, I'll take you home."

She spun round in her flowered dress, lace coiling in the air. "I don't need you. I can go home by myself." She clapped her hands over her ears, which were poking out from her neat hair. "It's noisy in here."

It was full of voices contained in a small space. The reverberations hurt me too. "I'm done here. I'm going," I told her.

"Can we play in the woods?" She grinned.

"Yes." I took her impatient hand. The forest with its indirect, apostatizing sounds beckoned. The noises of tiny animals, insects, twigs brushed aside, the solid anger of rocks, the way the sky spread out like a blue puddle. "I can't find what I'm looking for here anyway."

We left behind all the adult conversations, the polite inquiries about someone else's family, the intoning of the men's and women's voices. There weren't many children there. The little girl skipped ahead of me. I wasn't sure whether she would be benevolent or malevolent that day, maybe both. She was her own phenomenon like me. Her combed blonde hair wicked back and forth behind her in the wind and suddenly she disappeared. I grabbed a tree trunk and hurled myself forward to find her. It was the first time I had ever lost someone and it was a little blind girl. I searched in a grove of trees.

"Kat, Kat," I called.

Finally I heard giggling and found her in a clearing, the sun highlighting her sleek blonde hair, a yellow river. She was rolling in some high grass, her shoes off.

I was angry. "How did you get here so fast? How did you find your way?"

"I know these woods. I know all the paths through them." She was laughing, grass blades protruded from her hair.

"Rebellious." But it was enjoyable to hear her soft laughter. I found all those emotions confusing and mixed. I was relieved to find her.

"Do you want to play Doctor?" she asked me.

"What does it entail?"

"You take off all your clothes and I give you an exam," she said.

"Will there be operations?"

"Of course," she sat upright, using a deeper voice she said, "that's part of my job."

"Then no, I definitely don't want to play Doctor."

"You know I can't see you anyway," she sulked. "I can't see one naked bit of you," she emphasized.

"No, I said."

"What if you are the Doctor then?" She started to pull her nice dress off. "Then you can give me an exam."

"Is that what you were doing to poor Miss Moscovitz?"

Both of our heads turned as we heard a distinct snapping of branches to our right. I expected to see a swath of glistening blonde hair. I wasn't sure why. But it was black hair that appeared from behind a tree with that terrible smell. Then the man, Fred, lit half of a cigarette, contemplated us, and, snickering, moved closer.

"What are you girls doing?" the man stupidly asked.

"Fred!" Kat said with alarm. "You'd better not come near."

"Oh and why is that, little Katrina?" He inhaled and exhaled. Smoke somersaulted in the air. "Are you doing something you shouldn't be doing?"

The man was stuffed with silly questions. I didn't understand him. I remembered what Theresa told me. "Go away," I demanded.

"You're new here," Fred said. "Kat comes from an interesting family in these here parts, a father with a temper, a religious mother, and a brother who's supposed to be haunting these woods. Now, they say that Kat wasn't blind at birth. That something happened to her. Is that true Kat? What really happened?"

"I've been blind as long as I can remember." The little girl was confused and upset by the man. She began prancing in circles. "This is one of my favorite trees." She hugged a Ponderosa Pine.

"You can come back to my house with me, Kat. Hell, you can

live with me if you want to and get away from your crazy old mother. I have candy and horses to ride. You'd like it, living with me." The man was looking at me as he spoke. He smiled, and I saw that his teeth were rotting and brown. Entropy.

He walked closer to us. "Run," I whispered to Kat. She whisked her head in the direction of her house and began to move quickly but carefully. I scooped her in my arms and ran faster. His words ricocheted inside my hollow head. Everyone had a past. My past was just not singly my own. The man followed us, running behind me.

I stopped for a moment to hear if he was still behind me. He caught up with us swiftly. I was surprised.

"Hey, Mara, you're a big girl. Why stay with that crazy family? You should just leave. You can see that Peter's gone and you came here for him. Our town's done fine without you. Just collect your wash money and go. You don't want to get in the middle of something that isn't any of your business." He was right behind me. He reached out and touched my shoulder.

With my one arm cradling Kat I reached out my other arm and twisted his hand away. I heard his wrist snap. So did Kat.

She exclaimed, "Oh!"

I saw that I had rotated it. Fred crumpled to the ground and writhed in pain. I backed away from him and continued hurrying to the house. I could have fixed him a sling, having learned some things about the body from Father. But I ran.

"Goddamn bitch," he yelled, "I'll get you. I'll get you both. You'll see. You bitches can't get away from me." He lifted himself, but the hand was hanging.

I ran to the house, gently dropped the little girl inside and locked all the doors and windows. "You're home now, Kat."

"I know," she answered softly. "I can tell." She groped her way to a kitchen chair and sat. She cried little girl tears. "I can't help you fight Fred because I'm blind."

"Don't worry, Kat. I can take care of Fred." But I didn't want

111

to. I was made of dead people, but I didn't want to kill anyone.

I sat down at the kitchen table and waited. I closed my eyes.

I was a blind man in a rowboat out in the middle of a lake. The boat was going in circles. I could feel the boat spinning around, the current beneath me, the wood of the boat, the hard seat, the oars, my sunhat with a brim. I sniffed the murky, oily water, the blooming trees, even sensing when fish rose to the surface to inhale a bit of sky. A sandwich sat next to me, a thermos with coffee. I was fishing, but I hadn't thrown my line out. It was a distracted season, full of heat. I was thinking in circles about my family's debts. It didn't matter that I was blind. We needed to pay our bills. I didn't know what to do. I tried to sing a happy tune to make myself and the fish happy.

"What were you thinking about?" Kat asked. She shivered although it wasn't cold. "It was like you went somewhere else."

"I kind of did. Maybe it's more like being somebody else." It was quiet. No Fred banging at the doors, demanding to come in.

The little girl came over to me. She gently held my hand. I was afraid to move it or hold hers back.

"Thank you," she uttered softly.

"Befuddled," I gave her. I laughed my deep, mechanical laugh, dropping her hand.

"That's a funny word." The girl seemed surprised and then she laughed too. She had a light, tinkling, insubstantial little girl laugh.

Theresa unlocked the front door and entered. "Why are you girls laughing? And why is everything shut and locked?" She began opening the curtains and windows, allowing the inside air to argue with the outside air. An immense oak tree rose into view outside, but there was no man waiting there.

I was perplexed. Where was Fred? I stared outside and a clump of blonde hair was suspended in the architecture of one of the trees. When I looked again, it wasn't there. Fred had black hair. The colors in the kitchen became jumbled, yellow, brown, white. Chairs seemed to grow wings, tables hooves. The house was safe but suddenly strange.

Theresa snapped me out of my reverie. She turned and looked at us. "What's going on here?"

"Nothing," the little girl and I replied at the same time, not wanting to worry her.

♦ ♦ ♦ ♦ ♦

The next day I told Miss Elaina what had happened with Fred. I read to her about it from my notebook, which had once belonged to Sandy Shane. ". . . *a compilation of events beyond my understanding of them.* . . ."

Miss Elaina was disturbed. "That Fred is awful. Do you need my help, the sheriff's, or anyone else's?"

"No." I continued my reading.

Miss Elaina interrupted my reading, "Are you sure, Mara? Because you know we wouldn't mind helping Theresa and her family?"

"No, she is proud." I knew I could crush Fred if I had to. "We can take care of Fred if he bothers us again." I remembered Greg's body on Father's table.

"You saw blonde hair in the forest?"

"Yes. I think I did."

Her forehead became corrugated, as though she wasn't stitched together properly. Her white hair loosened from her bun, her eyeglasses slipped onto her nose. "You know there are so many stories about the forest." She smiled, "Most of them fabricated ages ago, and they don't mean anything." She frowned again. "But I do wonder what became of Peter, Theresa's son. No one knows where he is."

"Kat believes he's in the woods."

"That might explain some odd occurrences like food stolen

out of gardens and kitchens when no one's home. Sheds found rummaged, with tools missing. I couldn't find my purse one morning and when I found it underneath my couch, my money had disappeared." She pressed her lips together. "My window was open too. I thought I was just being forgetful."

"It's wrong to steal. But what if you need something to help you live? Then is it okay?" All the parts of others had their say.

Miss Elaina smiled her far away smile, the one she used when she was thinking about something else, something she wanted to share with me. My retrieving the laundry and delivering it to her house had become so much more.

"Let me show you a book." She rose and went to her library, my favorite room in her house.

I remained in the living room on the sofa, watching sunlight refracted through a glass cat with its clear haunches resting on a doily. The surprising colors crept across her table and I suddenly saw the memory of a young soldier with black skin. He carried a large rifle. He was sweating and jumping through some under-brush. He was terrified and yet smiling as he played some kind of a game with the leaves and soil, sticking his rifle into mounds of earth and stirring the ground. Then he was staring at me, pointing his rifle.

Miss Elaina returned carrying a book, Greek Mythology. She flipped through the pages. "Ah ha," she murmured. She handed the book to me. "Here's a section about Dryads, tree nymphs. They're very shy, except around Artemis, goddess of the hunt, animals, wilderness, virginity, and childbirth. Dryads live a long time and are connected to their trees. Maybe you saw a Dryad." She stretched her arm out, holding the large book.

"I don't know who or what I caught a glimpse of. But it doesn't seem to be a harmful spirit."

"Here, take this," she offered the book. "You can bring it back when you're done with it."

I smiled. "This is my first borrowed book from your library. I'll take good care of it." I stroked the thick book, resting next to me on Miss Elaina's sofa.

"Then you'll return it in perfect condition when you're done." It was an order, not a request.

"I would never steal it."

Miss Elaina turned her face so it was partially eclipsed by the room's shadows. "I don't know if I believe in wood nymphs, but stories about you are starting in this town. I wouldn't think much of it, though, since there's nothing here to do except gossip."

"What would anyone have to say?"

"Oh, you know, the usual things. That you're not a regular church-goer and therefore some kind of bad person."

"I went to church."

"But they didn't think you liked it there." Miss Elaina smiled and her eyeglasses slid further down her nose. Tendrils of white hair grappled at her neck. "I mentioned that I don't attend church at all. 'But,' they said, 'we've known you all your life.'"

"Mr. John Benjamin said that you changed his dog. Now he lets it run freely around his yard and it doesn't snap anymore. You're some kindred animal spirit, strong, too, for a girl."

"That's true. His dog, Calvin, was unhappy."

"Some people think you've bewitched the little blind girl, Kat, and her mother, so that you can stay with them. Other people wonder if you're a spy for a real estate company who wants to buy our land and build new houses here. Everyone has a theory."

"All I do is the laundry." I found her brown eyes lodged back behind her glasses. "You are apodictic."

"Thank you for the word. I know, I tell the truth. They're not used to outsiders here and no one believes the story about being a friend of Peter's. Did you really know Peter?"

"No. I wandered here and Theresa took me in." I saw yellow and blue emanating from Miss Elaina's skin as though she had dressed herself in colors this morning.

"Peter was a strange boy, almost a man at seventeen, when he disappeared. Everyone thought his father had something to do with it since they disappeared at around the same time. But then they found the father mauled by a bear. Peter never did return. Everyone figures he's living somewhere between here and the city. He probably has his own family by now. He could be dead in the woods, where no one can find him. Most young people leave this town and none of them ever come back except to visit." She peered intently at her beige carpet, shook her head, "I don't know what will happen with Kat."

"Theresa will protect her. She's her mother."

"Theresa can't always be there. Look at Fred. It was a good thing that you were there."

"He hasn't come to find us again."

"No one has seen him since church yesterday, which is strange, since he goes to the bar often."

"Hibernation," I offered.

Miss Elaina laughed. "He's not a bear. He's probably lying low right now. I can get the sheriff next week to look for him if I need to."

"I don't like him."

"No one does. As a town we try and take care of our own." Miss Elaina leaned over and tapped the mythology book. "You might find yourself in there. It seems like everyone is represented by some kind of archetype, beneficial or ominous or both."

"Who would you be in Greek mythology?"

"I would like to be Thalia, one of the Muses who inspire writers and artists." The calibrated sunlight through her window was beginning to fail, misplacing her collection of small objects.

I wanted to take her hand, but I was fearful of crushing it. "You are a good human being, Miss Elaina. I have enjoyed talking to you."

"You sound as if you are leaving. How is it living with Theresa?"

"Fine. I'm learning a lot," I explained to her.

"About laundry?" We both laughed.

Miss Elaina appeared startled. "That's quite a laugh you have."

◆ ◆ ◆ ◆ ◆

I was carrying laundry back to the house through the usual forest path. Several of my fingernails fell off, perhaps from rubbing and handling the laundry bags. I didn't care anymore. It didn't hurt much and there was hardly any blood. I abandoned the nails. I had a gravitational longing for leaves and logs. I wanted to sit, allow images unearthed from other people to arise in me, tell me stories while I delighted in the fields, rocks, and river alongside of me. There were so many different ways that I could learn about the world, my own experiences, the memories of others, stories, myths, books, Miss Elaina, Theresa, the study of one insect that was born over unnamed dark water, lived flagrantly, unbridled, for one day and then expired. The Culicid, which passed through all stages in their life cycle, egg, larva, pupa, and adult or imago so quickly. The insect would need to remember every detail, heartbreak, stars, rain, water and its waterness, existing flamboyantly before dying.

Instead of being contemplative I pushed myself on toward the house. As I neared the house I saw the little girl running in circles around the yard, squeaking out yelps. When I grew closer I noticed blood on the front of her shirt. I dropped the laundry and ran. Theresa reached her from the house about the same time I did.

Later I would write: *the odd girl was dazed, her feet continuously moving as if she was surrounding something so it couldn't escape. I was big and clumsy. If I touched her I could hurt her in her strange state. She was still a Childcloud and therefore fragile. Silver sparks galloped around my eyes.*

"What happened to you? What's the matter, Kat?" Theresa searched inside the girl's shirt for wounds, pulled her clean hand out. She removed Kat's shirt. Underneath there was a thin graying undershirt. "Where did this blood come from?" Theresa took a handkerchief and wiped a spattering of blood from the girl's hands.

The little girl was sputtering and upset. "Fred," was all she managed to say.

Theresa was furious. "What did he do to you?" She began to tug at the girl's pants and underpants.

"No, come Mama," the little girl found her mother's hand, led her toward the deeper forest.

"I'll kill him if he hurt you," Theresa said. "Come back in the house. Where are we going, Kat?"

"Come," the girl said. "I hear you, Mara. You come too." She gestured at me.

I followed. The little girl sniffed the air and made several sharp turns and brought us to a place with deep underbrush. She dropped onto her hands and knees. Suddenly I could detect it too, although my sense of smell had faded. It was the odor of blood, fresh and drying, skin torn loose, waste from the body that was expelled.

We grew closer. Then I saw it, Fred's mangled body. Theresa and I walked closer, pushed branches out of the way. The head and body had been damaged so that the inner organs and brain would have been useless to Father. It was a waste of his body. I briefly considered trying to use Fred's ear or disgusting teeth or fingers to replace my own. But I didn't know what to do and they had probably deteriorated too rapidly already.

"Repugnant," I said and turned away. "Abhorrent."

"I don't know what those words mean but this is awful. I don't know what to do," Theresa exclaimed. She sat down on some grass. "Did you hear anything, Kat?"

"No," the girl shook her head repeatedly. "I found him."

"Alright," Theresa said, looking at us both. "The whole town knows how much we disliked Fred. Go back home now, Kat, and take a bath. Mara and I will be there soon after we figure out what to do."

"Okay." The little girl solemnly began to return to the house. "But," she said over her shoulder, stopping, "I think a bear did it." Then she continued walking with her hands outspread along the path.

"Someone beat him from behind, his head and his legs, and then sliced selected parts of him open," I stated.

"You seem to know a lot about dead bodies."

"Someone dragged him here, near the house." I pointed to indentations along the shrubs and the scraping on the ground. "I can't tell from where. But there are footprints."

"Shit," Theresa uncharacteristically said.

"We are all deciduous," I told her, "congealing and uncongealing."

"I don't know what you're talking about half the time, but you're strong. Do you think you could lift him?"

"Yes. But he cannot be resuscitated."

"I didn't think he could be." She stared at the body. "Carry him, Mara, and follow me."

I did what she told me. "Malodorous," I repeated as I smelled everything he had been and everything that had escaped him. Blood stained my clothes. I was tired of being so close to death, including the extinction of someone I disliked, although I truly didn't mind Fred being dead and out of our lives.

"Throw him over there." She pointed to a slight clearing behind some trees.

His body landed and an intestine flung itself from a hole in his body. A patch of hair and skull escaped.

"Find a very sharp stick," she barked at me.

We both began searching for a good stick. Theresa found one. She approached the dead body and made deep gashes on his exposed flesh and on his shirt, one or two long ones on his legs.

"Perfect," she said looking at her handiwork. "They might think it was an animal, at least for a while."

"You have created a work of death," I complimented her. Not a work of life as Father had.

119

We cleaned the stick with our clothes and tossed it far into the woods. We picked up any stray pieces of Fred that had fallen off in his transfer and we brushed away any footprints and broken branches, rearranged crushed bushes. "Who did this and why did they leave Fred for us to find?"

"You didn't do it then." It was almost a question. "You could have." She hurried toward the house. "We need to make sure Kat is fine and burn all these clothes and take baths." She stopped, "No one must find out about Fred. This has to be our secret."

"I don't like secrets. And shouldn't we tell someone?"

"Someone will find him."

"At least now the girl will be safe."

"Yes," Theresa was smiling, "Kat will be fine. I don't have to worry about Fred anymore."

"That's good."

"If I were you I'd leave soon," Theresa explained. "Once they find Fred's body any outsider will be the first person they suspect. They saw you fighting with Fred at church."

"But I didn't do anything."

"I know," Theresa exclaimed gloomily, "but that's just the way things are in this town." Theresa took my hand, hers fitting neatly inside my large, disintegrating one. I was afraid to close it. "I'll miss you, Mara. You've been good to Kat, you're a hard worker, and you've helped me a lot. You're good deep down inside your enormous body." She glanced at the ground. "See, I've learned some new words from you."

♦ ♦ ♦ ♦ ♦

After all our thorough baths and after Theresa and I had burned our meager clothes I went outside to sit in the surly forest. I did find it interesting that the people I disliked had died, Fred, Greg. But it seemed merely coincidental.

"So much has happened out here," I whispered to the ferns and moss as I sat on a fallen tree trunk. This time I noticed rot on the tree trunks, the parasitic mushrooms, vines, and moss, and the way small green plants died and came back to life. Nature renewed itself, but not always. A flower's seeds could sprout several new ones before it curled up and blew away. Flower One was the source for Flowers Two, Three, and Four. Nature was not feeble, even when displaying delicate skeletal branches or arterial flower stalks. But the forest had seemed more beautiful to me before I discovered her inner workings. There were tricks of nature to achieving the ethereal loveliness of butterflies and insects and plants and a dark side to sustaining their survival. Decomposition and decay lay the foundation for growth and it was happening all the time, alongside birth, death, blooms, leafing, fertilization, churning, watering. But the forest was sullen, aggravated at the constant changes. It was growing tired. I was, too.

In this memory a clown with a red bulbous nose, overlarge shoes, baggy clothes, a white face, red mouth, and a large, floppy hat stomped toward me. I smiled. I was frightened. The clown seemed friendly and funny. I knew that deep inside he was angry. His gestures were dramatic as he blew up a yellow balloon, his white gloves clutching the inflating rubber between his red lips. He pulled the balloon away and held it aloft, gave a grin like one I had seen on Fred.

"For the birthday girl." He smirked and held out the yellow circle to me that tried to fly away.

I must have screamed because someone was covering my mouth with a hand. I almost ripped it from my mouth. Then I smelled him behind me. His scent was the forest, blending in with trees, flowers, moss, earth, but he also smelled of blood and something charred, anger. I hadn't heard him. He moved in front of me quickly, before I could injure him, the boy with a shock of blonde hair.

"You were calling for your father." He blinked at me, at my

121

size, even though I was sitting. "You don't have to worry about Kat. I'll take care of her." His clothes were tattered. He was dirty and unruly and he looked a lot like the little girl.

"Isn't that Theresa's job?"

"Yeah, but I know you've been helping her and Theresa gets busy." The boy sat down next to me as though he knew me already. He seemed comfortable. "You're really big up close. I've only seen you from a distance."

"You watch over us?" I had seen glimpses of him in the woods.

"Yeah."

"Who are you?" But I already knew.

"Peter."

"Why are you living in the woods?"

"I'm a hunter, like my father. I'm not interested in human company."

"What happened to Fred?"

"I killed him."

We both paused, concentrating on that fact. Trees bent in the wind as though they were nodding.

"What happens when people die?"

The boy surveyed the woods around him. "They become part of the forest."

"That isn't what Theresa says."

"She's got religion. It didn't do Fred much good. He was on his way to our house. I wouldn't let anyone harm my family."

"It's wrong to kill someone."

"Even if someone wants to kill you or the people you love?" He shook his head and tentacles of greasy blonde hair stuck to the sides of his head.

I wondered how I would have felt if Greg had killed Father instead.

Peter didn't care what I thought. He snarled at something far away that I couldn't see, but I could hear it, a shrill, high, piercing noise.

"My father killed people too," I confessed to the wild boy.

"I killed my father," the boy from the wilderness said and then he disappeared.

◆ ◆ ◆ ◆ ◆

"I saw Peter," I told the little girl that night in our cramped bedroom.

"I told you he was out there." Her blank eyes were intent on my voice. "He takes care of me."

"Yes, you're right. You don't have to worry."

The little girl gathered her sheets and covers, turned onto her side, stayed very still and quiet.

◆ ◆ ◆ ◆ ◆

I returned Miss Elaina's Greek mythology book, which was still in pristine condition, leaving it on her porch in the early morning, before we left. The dawn light was frail company compared to Miss Elaina. I wished I could talk to her again. I wanted to discuss the Greek gods. But I didn't want to disturb her sleep. What would the gods have made of Fred's death, Peter, Kat, Theresa? I thought of Pegasus, a winged horse who brought lightning and thunder from the heavens and helped writers. He also became a constellation, who could guide me as I made my way farther into the world.

"We are homologous," I whispered to her front door, really meaning that we were friends. I slipped a note that claimed: *'The past is never dead. It's not even the past.' said by William Faulkner* into the first page of the book. I also tucked a story randomly into the book.

The Story of Sight

The little girl was growing mechanical in her despair at seeing the future. She felt composed of cogs, wheels, metal parts that ran but gave nothing more. She wanted nature, with its dark cloud confections, clutching trees, soft grass. She hoped her constant feeling of dread would soon disappear. Birds fell into her arms in their weariness with her visions of what was to come. The girl was lifeless at school, at home, at her tasks. She knew too much for her age. She carried the weight of the world, peeling back sky to expose stars, circling a spot of earth until it was comfortable. People pestered her about money, love, health. They propped her eyelids open so she could foretell more. At night her mind bloomed with predictions and she couldn't sleep.

"Write down what you see about what's forthcoming," the dragonfly, her friend, beseeched her.

"If I don't write it down, maybe it won't come to pass," the little girl answered.

"No," the wise dragonfly said, "you can't stop anything from occurring. You can only warn us."

But the little girl didn't want to see all those ghosts in the woods or all the different places her mind travelled to. She didn't want all that responsibility. She liked the empty darkness. So she fell on some rocks and blinded herself. The little girl hoped then that all the people would leave her alone. I'm useless to them, she thought. She could still feel the sky being shaped by gods who beat the air with their large wings and she didn't know what they would think about her blindness.

"What did you do?" shrieked the dragonfly when he saw her blank eyes.

"I'm making a new world," the girl said, "one without me."

"But without your sight you can see more," the dragonfly explained. "It was always about what was contained in your mind and the world will need you more than ever now."

Part III

The City

Chapter Nine

Mack's truck rattled along the highway, bouncing Theresa, the little girl, me, and the load of equipment tied down in the back. It was noisy inside and out. I tried to cover my ears with my hands. I didn't like the clamor and discord. I was nervous and elated about the city. I wore my washed and patched clothes, repaired shoes. I carried my notebook, tucked away in a sweater pocket.

Theresa had handed me the $110 she discovered in my clothes before she washed them. I placed the money in my pants pocket. "I want to give you some money for helping me too," she said.

"I'm not interested in money," I told her. "You and Kat need it." I tried giving her my $110, but she wouldn't accept it. "Kat will be happy to have the room to herself now."

"She's fond of you, Mara."

"Obstinate," I told myself to keep the sounds away.

I had all the possessions I needed. One of my kidneys had stopped working and an eyebrow had peeled off that morning. I looked less human, battered, large, and distorted. Colors whisked by, cramming themselves into my eyes. I was relieved to be reaching the mythical city before my body completely fell apart in front of Theresa and Miss Elaina. The little girl wouldn't care since she couldn't see me anyway, although she could sense so much. In the city I could be unknown and unnoticed.

After several hours the houses grew closer to one another and the traffic denser. We reached cement streets, tall buildings, buses. We parked near some cars on a busy street. I finally removed my hands from my ears. Then I wanted to clap them back on. A continuous roar filled my ears, honking, conversations, doors opening and closing, cars following one another.

"The noise'll hurt for a while and then go away when you get used to it." Theresa patted my arms.

"I'll get used to it?"

She nodded.

We all left the truck. I was the only one not returning. Theresa took Kat's small hand. Stores lined the streets and were filled with people searching for what they needed. Mack slipped into one of the larger stores with neon signs and equipment stuffed into the front window. I studied people as quickly as I could, but they were hurrying. None resembled Theresa, Kat, Mack, Miss Elaina, or me. Many were dressed in their Sunday clothes and anxious to get somewhere without seeing or hearing anything that would stop them along the way. I breathed a sigh of relief because none of them would notice me, even if I was taller than most of them.

Theresa kissed me on my cheek and handed me a piece of paper. "This is my cousin's address here in case you need it." Everyone left me standing, perplexed, in the middle of the street with people eddying all around me. I knew I had to pretend to be going somewhere in the huge, dissonant city.

♦　♦　♦　♦　♦

The city was a living organism, like the forest, that disintegrated and tried to reconstitute itself. I jumped into the back of a bus along with several other people when it opened an accordioned door. People helped me figure out my change for the fare box although they were reluctant to touch the coins in my palms. The driver handed me leaflets about city routes and pointed to his signs. I didn't care where I was going. A stream of advertisements flowed above our heads. I saw myself reflected in the bent steel over a wheel, and I was a large wardrobe filled with a disheveled woman. No one sat near me. I watched the disinterested people inside, reading a newspaper, lost in their own thoughts, looking out a window, quiet and pensive. Then I watched the streets surrounding the buildings and the people that navigated them. There was an endless supply of every kind of person. I felt alone without Theresa, Kat, even Mack or Peter. No one knew me although I was swimming around people.

"Anonymous," I whispered to myself. I knew I could go anywhere, do anything. The forest still lived inside me, as did all the other Maras. The bus passed places I could have stopped and lived in, apartments with laundry hanging from balconies or tall plain buildings with empty basketball courts and weeds growing through the sidewalks. I wondered what Father was doing now, working, or downstairs in the lab, or making his own dinner? I had seen enough of the city from the bus, a museum, the opera house, a department store all lit up and full of extravagant merchandise, the small pathetic trees that seemed to apologize to the wind. I began to feel at home in this constant sea of people. After all, what was I made of?

The bus driver's face studied me in the mirror that faced back, but he didn't say anything. I slipped off the back of the bus after memorizing its route, which looped three times around the city and its sliding, filthy river. I entered the nearby cavernous subway that echoed when feet rushed through there, a stampede of people at certain hours. I consulted a pamphlet, understood money and change and barely fit through the turnstile. I had a vague idea of where I wanted to go. A train surged by, its wind brushing my hair away from my disintegrating face. Another train roared by soon after. Its doors slid open, and I was thrust inside, along with a crowd of people. Everything clamored underneath the sidewalks. I could hear every conversation, every bit of clanging and noise from the trains. The new sounds were overwhelming. I slapped my hands over my ears as the subway train squealed at a turn. Fluorescent lights blinked on and off. Although it was well lit inside the subway cars, the passageways were dark and arterial. The map that showed how they ran beneath the skin of the city was multicolored and splayed in front of my face. Sometimes it resembled one of my bad dreams, but I was learning the city inside and out. It reminded me of my own body, sections and transportation centers that functioned as legs and arms, government offices that were brains, the mouths of restaurants, the ears of antennae and satellites, the windows and video devices that were eyes. It was familiar, the construction and reconstruction done by men and machines, stops that released you, allowed you to return to the outer surface of skin again.

"Greg, you're a naughty boy," I overheard someone scolding a child, who was holding a stuffed dog in a seat across from me. My head snapped toward them.

Then, under the harsh light, our plastic seats vibrated as the train hurried along the tracks until it abruptly stopped and threw its doors open again. I closed my eyes.

"I'm coming around to your way of thinking," I said. I was a slim woman with black shimmering hair and boiling eyes. I wore red lipstick. I was gripping a handrail by the steps on a shaking, speeding railroad train. I was near the threshold that separated the train from the outside world. My hair flew every which way.

"I need to live as much as I can to make up for the lives of the others that were lost in the war," the man with an extraordinary nose said. He was terribly handsome. He thrust his head out, past the train steps, into the green and brown landscape which we were speeding by. "Let's see what's out there for us." The wind pushed his features askew.

"The world is free," I answered him.

"As it should be." I think he said.

The man took my hand in his and we looked at one another.

The wind stole our endearments on the steps. I knew I would follow him wherever he went although I didn't always agree with him. We jumped off the train together. He rolled past some grass into a ditch. I landed on some rocks, and I could hear my bones breaking.

I opened my eyes, exiting haphazardly where the train stopped. The sign proclaimed RANDOM STREET STATION. I had a headache from the lights, the noise. Vortexes of dust spiraled into dancing esophagi on the cement ground as I rose onto the streets. I missed the affection of animals and stared at a small black and white dog and the elderly woman owner walking and halting at a fire hydrant. Sirens blared while the rumbling and honking of vehicles seemed incessant. I smelled fried food, perfume, cake, coffee, bread, soap, flowers. The air was dirty. There were too many odors. I had to strain them, simplify them, toss them aside. I grew hungry and my leg muscles stiffened, my gait becoming a lurch. Red and black began to swirl around my head and bright silver sparks circled it like a tiara.

"Olfactory, permeable imposter," I whispered to myself as I fell through a maze of city streets into a park that was more decorous and tame than the forest. I found some gnawed donuts, a half empty soda, and a peanut butter sandwich in a trash can. I sat behind some benches and ate greedily.

A family walked by with a child in a stroller who pointed at me and laughed, mewling, "Monster girl."

Her mother tapped the child's tiny finger, said, "Don't be rude."

But I agreed with her. I was scatterbrained, brokenhearted, a Mara surfeit, and I didn't have any plans on how to survive in the city. I could contact Teresa's cousin. I reached into my pocket and discovered that I had lost the piece of paper Teresa had given me with the address. I probably misplaced it in the subway. I crawled back towards some bushes. It was becoming dark and some streetlights began to glow, the sound of footsteps and wheels on the pavements lessened. Fewer cars streamed by on a road past the far trees; their headlights were caught in the burgeoning tree branches and turned over by the green leaves. It grew peaceful in a strange, intrusive way. I curled under a bare bush, the ground was still warm and the grass flattened. I fell asleep.

"You're becoming obsolete," Father said. "See," he stated, pointing out my detached knee cap that had no place to go. Then he inspected my ears, eyebrows, ferreting out missing fingers and toes with his eyepiece that enlarged what he saw. "What's next to go?"

"I don't know." I was sullen. "Did you give my parts expiration dates?"

He laughed. "You have a good sense of humor."

"It's better than yours, apparently." I tapped the pocket on his white coat, found the edges of his Photographs. But when I removed them to study the Mother, Daughter, and the Scientist in their usual poses I discovered that the pictures had been torn into small pieces. So the arms, legs, necks, heads, and torsos of each person were all jumbled and mixed up with each other. I lay the parts out on the operating table and tried to reassemble them into the original Photographs. As I grew close to finishing one person, I'd find an extra piece of an arm or a hat or too much hair, so I couldn't complete even one that was exactly the same as my memory of it. I became frantic.

Father lay his hand on mine, calming my nervous fingers. "Things change."

"I don't like this." I glanced at my remaining toes as though they were disappearing as we spoke, three, two, one. "Why? Why am I coming apart? Why am I becoming invisible?"

"Ha, ha," Father bellowed. "Now I've created the Invisible Woman."

"It isn't funny." I was sulking.

"You've always known that the body parts could only last so long." He removed his eyepiece. "I need to replace them periodically. You already know where they come from. You remember Greg."

"I need a carapace."

132

"It wouldn't stop the process. And you wouldn't be human."

"Vicissitude," I gave him.

"Agglutinative problems," he countered.

"Synaesthesia," I volleyed. "Harmony between all the parts," I bowed my head as if I was praying. We were getting technical.

"I can fix you if you let me. You know that," Father said. "Just look around the room."

It was then that I noticed all the dead bodies piled up everywhere, surrounding our feet. Bodies of women, mostly, lined the laboratory floors, curled in every corner, stacked up against the walls. In some places they were a few rows deep. Their open eyes stared at me, their limbs flopped and useless. Several children and men were randomly included. I suddenly smelled them, a slight rotting mixed with form-aldehyde, the newly dead.

"Where did you find so many bodies?" I was stunned.

Father flipped his hand, undid his eyepiece. "Mara, people die all the time."

I leaned down, touched the cold, stiff arm of a young woman in an orange dress with dark hair who lay straight as a board on top of an older woman on her side, curved into a parenthesis. "I don't want their parts." I was disgusted.

"Maybe I need to try a new method," Father was thinking out loud, "cloning or some other type of regeneration. Like this," Father opened one of his hands in my dream and a tiny embryo, an unborn human, appeared in his palm. When he poked it with his finger to turn it over, the embryo peered at me with my face.

◆　◆　◆　◆　◆

I woke to a man's flaccid penis in my face. He smelled of liquor, greasy food, urine, vomit, and other bodily functions. The zipper on his pants was open. He looked worse than Greg, disassembled on my father's operating table. He had dirty hair and bad breath. I didn't look that good either.

"I bet you want this," he wiggled his wormy penis in the air.

He was straddling upright over me in a way I didn't like, falling to one side or the other as though he couldn't stay perpendicular. I brushed the hair from my face, saw he had his penis in one hand and a bottle of something in his other hand, waving both uncontrollably. "No, I don't," I stated, dirt flying from his scuffing feet near my face.

"Ugh," he stopped his tipping. "You're butt ugly." He smiled, and he had numerous teeth missing. "But that's okay. I don't need to look at no face, you know what I mean." He winked and began pulling at my pants and clothes.

"You're annoying me," I warned him. He managed to pull down my pants a bit before I sat up, knocking him aside, stretching my arms. I lay back down again.

"Whoa, things aren't right down there"—he was pointing at my stomach and my sexual parts—"unless I'm just too damn drunk." He smiled his hideous smile. "Oh shit, that's okay. I don't care." He rose and started fumbling with my clothes again.

"Just stop it," I exclaimed loudly. "I don't want your penis."

"You got money?" He was kneeling over me and mumbling, "'cause I need money too."

Streetlights were fading and sunlight was beginning to caress the horizon. I couldn't stand the smell of him, his dirty hands searching my clothes, the spilled liquor, his filthy penis flapping against my legs. I stood up, displacing him. He fell onto the earth with a thud; his bottle emptied as it rolled away. I arranged my clothes.

He looked up at me. "Shit, you're one big lady." He sat and grabbed his bottle. He shook it. "It's gone. See what you did. Now you owe me." He threw the hollow bottle aside, stood next to me, his fists balled.

"Go away," I ordered him. "I don't like you."

"Nobody tells me what the fuck to do," he yelled. He ran at me in wobbling circles and started pounding my arms, where he could reach them.

I was afraid he would knock more parts off of me so I picked him up by the back of his shirt. His body was hollow, empty, and lightweight. I flung him away. He hit a tree and skidded down the trunk with his eyes closed. He fell onto his side among some flowers and bushes. I went over to him, felt his pulse and checked his nostrils for breath. I checked my pants pocket for my money and it was still there. A tattered woman ran to me. She imitated my medical gestures.

"Shit," she said, "he's still alive." Her round face scurried out from her bundle of rags. She smiled. Her rotten teeth reminded me of brown butterflies shyly revealing themselves. She was dissolving into her old, raggedy clothes the same way I was losing pieces of myself. "But I like your style and I could use some protection around here." She snuffled, wiped her nose with a torn sleeve. She looped one arm around mine. She was wearing woolen gloves. "You're new here, ain't you?"

I nodded, looking around. I was in a public park. Early morning joggers and people hurrying to work were passing us by along the sidewalks. We were invisible. She, at least, smelled better than the man.

"I'll show you the ropes, Honey."

"Conspiratorial." I gave her a word for the manner in which she was addressing me.

The horrible man on the ground began moaning.

"Ignore him. We call him Benjie 'cause he's a lot like a bad dog." She laughed, and I thought that she might lose some of her teeth from the gasping and jerking.

I laughed with my grinding noise, to be polite. "Maybe I should help him up?"

"Naw," she said, "he'll just start bothering you again." She stepped away from me and formally held out her purple, gloved palm. "My name's Misty. You'll need a name here, Hon, just so people will know you by something. You can make up whatever name you want." She looked me up and down, "How about

Crow? Your face and everything's coming apart. You're dark and big." She gently patted my arm.

"I'll think of a name," I told her, happy to name myself, like being too tired to wake in the morning and then suddenly discovering some energy, like being reborn.

Benjie was hunched over a cigarette, his face scraped by the tree, the clear bottle lolling by his sad shoes. He had settled himself in the bushes and was squinting up at the tree tops, as if there was a full liquor bottle in the sky and he was figuring out how to drink the distance. Smoke circled his annoying head.

"Screw him," Misty said. "I'll show you the sights in this city." Misty scrounged in some bushes and pulled out a shopping cart filled with a baby's green chair, a book with curled pages, bronze ballet shoes, a red long-haired wig hanging over the side. "This here's my best friend." She slapped the cart. "She goes where I go."

"I've been on the #18 bus and taken the subway too." I spread out my arms and some joggers on the path ran to the other side of the road.

"You ain't seen nothing yet." She smiled her decaying apple smile. She held out her purple gloved hand. "Shake my hand and we got a deal to take care of each other."

I slipped my hand into her scratchy purple one and it moved up and down. "Tentative," I gave both of us.

"Yeah, whatever," she said.

Chapter Ten

The city reared up and took a hard look at me. It was an appraising city and what it saw was a large, lost girl/woman, lonely in the way solitary people can be lonely. I was a curious person who wanted to carve a chosen life amid the fumes of dust, smoke, cars, and tall buildings. Misty showed me mazes under the concrete, gaping holes that become filled with plant and human life, foul, strange places full of strangers and others who were homeless. They convened around smashed, abandoned cars, under bridges, in the backs of restaurants and department stores, under cardboard boxes, sometimes finding the occasional good luck of a decrepit building or bankrupt motel. We kept our distance from the people who were reassured and distracted in their lives, the ones going to work, busy with their children, people who couldn't conceive of not having a home or living out of a shopping cart. We were the faces that everyone saw, but no one could remember.

We had to leave her shopping cart in the corner of a subway stop, well-hidden underneath the stairs in Misty's safe place, while we took a train to a beach that skirted the profile of the city. At first I thought it was a wasteland. There were no trees. Birds passed over the odd, pale stretch of glassy substance that was warm and reflected sunlight: sand at the shore. I had seen pictures. It was not at all like soil. I allowed the granules to run through my injured fingers. Suddenly I had a memory of sand, tiny grains of disintegrated and worn rock, elemental and refigured. Stones jutted out into the water, which wrinkled up into white-topped waves that ran toward the shore. Families were screaming, dipping their toes in the water, playing with balls. I didn't understand what the beach's purpose was. An old couch and broken bottles, along with crushed soda and beer cans, lined the edges. I smelled salt, fish, suntan oil, sweat, and something murky and unnamable. We sat on a crumbling wall watching a hot dog vendor zigzag through the people, towels, and umbrellas. A father, fighting with his wife, was shaking his fist at his children; one was a deformed teenager, pouring water from a bucket onto her head for no apparent reason.

I pointed her out to Misty. "Are there many people like that?" I noticed her dark hair, darting eyes, her features falling into one another. I felt my partial ear, scanned my missing fingers, remembered my severed toes, askance eyebrow. My right elbow was cracking. The girl's mouth was distorted and she wore a questioning look on her face. Her limbs were beyond her control. But we were alike in some way I couldn't describe.

Misty nodded. "Enough."

Vagrant sunlight flew into the young girl's face and she crossed her arms, shielded her wet cheeks. She resembled a dog, studying her family, wondering what they would do next, having no idea why anyone would do such a thing. The girl collapsed into a sitting position and continued following her parents' argument, while the remaining bored and restless children scattered toward the water.

"Oh, for a box of childhood," Misty moaned as we sat, spreading out our clothes along the wall full of beach rubble. She was watching me watching the young girl.

"I was once a Childcloud like that," I confessed. The odd young girl was standing upright, flapping her arms as if she wanted to fly somewhere else. I wrote in my hidden notebook, *Provocative.*

"I don't know what to do with her either," the girl's mother screamed so loudly at the father that we could hear them clearly above the din and murmur of everyone else and the waves with their little, white slurping sounds.

It was hot and made me think of all the various ways our bodies leave us. How thoughts passed through the body, not circumventing it, changing it. How, in the humidity and heat, another body could form.

"My intentions are parked somewhere and you're inside them," Misty whispered to me.

"I'm developing my interior," I tried to explain to her.

"There's a circus in the clouds." She pointed out over the water, and I could almost see a Ferris wheel or fluffy acrobats in the sky. She cupped her ear, hidden under her knit hat, with her purple, gloved hand, "I can hear birds barking answers."

"Instead of wanting to be loved, maybe now I want to love." I was trying to be reasonable. A blossom of sunlight crawled along my sleeve.

She turned toward a washer that was gutted and rusting behind us. "Bruises can be worn outside our clothing," she told the machine.

"Misty, I don't understand what you're saying and I keep trying." Her head swiveled toward me.

I was still spying on the family. The father grabbed the girl's arms and held them close to her body. The girl was beginning to explode. She had turned red, her eyes were squinting, and her torso trembled.

After a few minutes she screamed, "Argh" over and over.

"Oh my God, she's babbling again," the mother said. Her hand slapped the girl's mouth and then fell to her side. The girl was quiet again. They released her arms and began packing all their beach belongings.

"C'mon kids, we're going," the father yelled at the other wayward children.

"That's because today doesn't say the same thing it did yesterday." Misty was talking to a large rock sitting near us on the wall.

"That's because all my meds are in my cart, which is disguised as a cloud in the hereafter. Watch out for it!"

The family hurried away, sand spitting behind them. The mother towed the girl, holding onto her clothes, said to the father, "She's a disaster today."

Misty stared at me. "You're a refrigerator so stop talking to me."

Misty was making contorted faces, one after another.

"We need to get you back to your shopping cart." I rose. I took her arm and gently pulled her along. "I found my new name. It's Refrigerator," I told her.

♦　♦　♦　♦　♦

Misty and I retraced our steps and found her hidden shopping cart underneath the subway stairs where we had left it. I was relieved when she dug out a bottle of pills and swallowed some without water. We sat on a cement bench until her face relaxed, her breath no longer so exasperated, her heart rate slowing. It was beginning to match the arrival and departure of the hurtling trains, whose wind brushed dirt, candy wrappers, and warm air against our skin. I realized that not only was I disassembling but that people were disintegrating all around me. And neither Father nor I had anything to do with it.

Misty smiled with her brown teeth. "Here," Misty said, thrusting the pill bottle toward me. "You look like you could use some of these."

"I was . . . concerned." I pushed the bottle away.

"Aw, c'mon. You might as well try 'em. I have tons."

My remaining eyebrow inched across my forehead. "What are they?"

"Don't know." She smiled again and I had to look away. "But I feel good. Go on, try it." She tossed one pill into my hand.

"Just one, then we need to find someplace to sleep."

"The park again? Or would you like something more . . . fancy?" She was rearranging her striped scarf.

"Cornucopia," I gave her.

Misty rolled her eyes. "Did you take it?"

"Yes, I swallowed it. I've taken a large assortment of pills in my past."

"Do you have any of them now?"

"No. I haven't had any operations recently."

"What's the matter with you?"

A bone in my wrist appeared to be floating around the river of my forearm. "The same as everyone."

"Oh." Misty spied something under a bench at the subway station. It was a small pillow, losing its stuffing and embroidered with a white cat on the front. "What a treasure!" she screeched.

"Equivocal," I gave her.

She studied me, tucking the pillow under the red wig draped on her cart.

"Pugnacious," I tried. She appeared flummoxed. We weren't speaking the same language. "Why can't two human representatives communicate?" I thought of Gloves and how we had managed to understand each other, using gestures. I tried to describe the word by punching at the air. I could feel a tiny bone crack into pieces under my left shoulder, which fell slightly down and forward. It hurt for a moment, then the pain flew away.

Misty stepped away from me and threw her arms into the air. Her raggedy sleeves hung down and swayed. She crossed her arms over her face as though I was going to hit her. "You're a freaking disaster."

A police officer sauntered into our dark corner. I could feel the metal-filled breeze as trains and people came and went. I could taste and smell all of humanity and the human world they built with its degrees of sweetness and bitterness in the dust and breath all around me. Misty and I were among the few stranded stragglers who neither arrived nor exited. Misty shrank into her torn clothes and shuffled behind her cart.

"Getting carried away here, aren't we, Ladies?" He was young, blonde, in the usual blue uniform, and he concentrated on me. "What's going on? Are we having a fight?" He shimmered in and out of the blinking overhead and train lights.

"Naw, fuck, Refrigerator," Misty managed, fading further into the darkness behind her cart.

I stepped closer toward him, unsure what I wanted to do, toss him onto the train tracks, hurry up the stairs and disappear, crush him, kiss him. Misty was right about the pill. I did feel better, as though I was seeing my life occur through a large bowl of water. Events were drifting, tossed onto one another, circles reverberating between them, viewed at such a great distance that they seemed unimportant. I could do anything.

I stumbled toward the officer. He twirled me around and quickly and expertly locked my wrists behind me in handcuffs. "You're big and unruly," he tilted his head up, toward me. I could see his disgust.

"Can I come too?" Misty asked. She whispered to me, "The grub's no good but it's not a bad place to sleep." She tucked her companion, the shopping cart, underneath the stairs.

She was growing more rational while I grew unrational. "All my bones did was ask."

"Come on, Ladies, time for a little rest." He led us out of the cavernous, noisy subway and into his well-lit patrol car. He had to tuck the height of me inside.

"I'm what's between the subway and clouds." I wanted to point at the sky. I wanted to tear the metal handcuffs apart and throw them on the floor. I pressed my lopsided face against the car window. It was as familiar as water. I was too scorched by the pill to do anything. At the police station, swarming with men just like him, the young policeman jostled us through procedures which tried to replicate our fingerprints.

"You still have a few fingers left," a middle-aged woman commented as she pressed the rind of my remaining fingers onto ink and then paper.

"Accidental afflictions. Did you want my mechanical arms?" I inquired as the woman frowned at me. "Or the small splashy fingerprints of raindrops?"

"Here," Misty offered her hands, "I can do it for both of us."

"Names?" the woman asked, cringing.

"Misty Me," Misty pointed to herself and the woman wrote it down.

"Re . . ." I trailed off, "frig . . . er . . . ator."

She started to write and then she looked at me, her auburn hair coiffed and unmoving under her hat. "Is Refrigerator your first or last name?"

"Querulous invertebrate." I tried to stampede her with words I knew she wouldn't understand.

Then I wouldn't allow them to photograph me. "Father wouldn't like it." I tried to accordion the camera between my palms but I had lost my strength and any will to finish the deed. Two policemen started to restrain me until I promised not to destroy the camera.

They released my arms, said "If you act up we'll put you in detention until we feel like letting you out."

I stepped back, encouraging them to photograph Misty, whose face, out of her hat, resembled gelatinous fruit. I wouldn't become a Photograph on anyone's wall, except, maybe, Father's.

There was an ordinary velocity to the events at the station. "There's someone else in the body I want. It's a penalty. Maybe later it could be a crime. What would you call it?" I asked the policeman.

"Disturbing the peace and disorderly conduct, a possible assault. And that's not even counting whatever drugs you two are on."

"How about my history at the house of meat and mistakes?" It must not have counted because his face showed no emotion. "Besides she's not pressing any charges." I pointed at Misty, who was grimacing at the camera. "No photographs," I screamed.

"We'll do it later when she's come down off of whatever she's on," the policeman mumbled to the photographer, as he showed us to our cells.

In the hallway I balked at the tiny, gray cage that reminded me of Father's research animals. I wondered if the small space I viewed could contain me. I studied the cement walls settling around me, the wide bars on the door, like bones pondering the addition of flesh, muscle, skin to become some new form of life. "What is the basis of this cell's intelligence?" I asked him just before I ducked into the cell and he locked me inside. It reminded me of something I had once overheard Father say.

It was a small, simple space and the height and breadth of me took up most of it. Against all that gray night peeked in through the window bars and colors corrupted me. They flowed everywhere, inside my head, down my throat, swirling near the close walls of my cell. Bright blue, red, yellow streaks surrounded me, tried to clothe me, then expanded within my interior. My perception was exhausted. I sat on a cot with a gray and white striped blanket. It was warm and a sparrow thumped inside my chest. I wondered what percentage of me was an accident and what percentage was planned by Father. I could hear others in their cells breathing, the clicking of keys on chains, the city outside the window with music leaking in from somewhere, a man saying to another, "Sometimes they ask too many questions." I could hear Misty humming nearby.

I was a woman made of dead people, dead daughters, dead mothers, dead homeless drifters and dead wealthy people. Old and young. Dead sisters. Dead wives. Anyone who could offer a body part I needed. The manufactured dead. All expendable. I wanted to howl like an animal, feel that sound ripping through my throat. The pain. So I did, bellowing through the bars of my cell.

"Shut the fuck up," Misty growled from her own cell.

A policeman came, who looked like all the others. Policeman One, Two, Five, a compilation of those who went before him. He stared at me through my bars. "Tomorrow, showers for you girls." But, by then, I was sitting down on my cot sedately, looking at a wall. He left.

"What is absolutely necessary?" I whispered to myself. I tried to pull the bars of my door, but they didn't budge. My arms were too weak. "How much longer does this pill last?" I asked in Misty's direction.

Inside lights went out, and I could hear footsteps fading away. "You'll be fine tomorrow morning," Misty said.

I smelled the stench from leftover lumps of food, vestiges of pork and beans and spinach. My stomach almost turned. Then I received a memory. I wished I could will the remembrances and dreams to explain certain things but I couldn't control them, at least not yet.

"I don't know how to build a life from what's left of this civilization," the young man with wild, dark hair and thick eyeglasses said to the beautiful young dark-haired woman who had a child growing inside of her.

The woman took his hand, "The war hasn't taken that much away from us." She placed his hand on her stomach.

The man smiled with straight, white teeth. "We could go elsewhere. I could concentrate on my research."

"We could go anywhere," she beamed at him. "I mean, I would go anywhere with you."

They rested on a bench inside a city park, looking at each other and listening. Musical instruments played in the distance. There was clapping from a large audience. Tree branches reminded her of hands making gestures. Fountains bubbled with water, children on bicycles rode by on paths that rose toward an unbroken, blue sky. A squirrel, a spasm of gray, ran past them.

The man patted her hand. "Encumbrance," she gave him.

But the man shook his head, "No, never." He turned his head toward her. "Resplendent," he gave her.

The woman lit up inside. "Thank you for the word." She smiled, a leaf slipping from its green hinge on a tree above her head, slowly somersaulting downward. Her face turned upward, toward him. "You can call me Mother from now on."

A patient smile curled on the man's lips. "Just call me Father."

My eyes, when they opened, searched around the dark cell, unable to see much of anything; my body, even full of various disagreeables, had remembered. I couldn't imagine Father married, but I knew he had been. The people in the Photographs had once been alive. I grew sad. I knew there was so much inside of me, so many lives, behind disgust, fear, and sadness. I discovered another feeling, anger. Too much injustice had happened to me.

A deep darkness permeated my cement cell and I wanted to scream. So I howled again, nothing intelligible, just an animal syllable for hurt. I howled as loudly as I could for as long as I could until my throat was raw and something inside of it shifted. I couldn't hear anyone or anything in the dark, quiet night.

Misty and the others inside their cells kept on saying things like, "C'mon stop it." "Nobody cares and nobody's coming." "Shut the fuck up so I can get to sleep," until they, too, grew tired and stopped trying to reason with me.

The world removed what I had loved bit by bit: Gloves, curiosity, learning, experience, parts of me. I wasn't what the world had wanted. A rampage was building up inside of me to take back what I had been promised, my own life. I had never killed any of them. They had done that to each other.

Memories, stories, and dreams created my skin, and kept me wandering. "Peregrination," I told myself. I tried to write in my notebook, hidden deep inside my clothes but I couldn't. I finally fell asleep.

I was screwing in a new arm I had found abandoned on a counter at a vacant department store in the city. It was a lovely dream in which

I could find everything I wanted. I was drifting down the streets, full of stores with delicate, ancient embellishments and lettering in a language I didn't understand. I squeezed and relaxed the fingers on my new arm as I strolled. I found food, left on a table at an empty restaurant. It was delicious, unlike the tasteless wad of food on a tray that one of the policemen had shoveled into my cell earlier. I saw my reflection in a women's clothing store window and I was restoring myself to my old looks, slowly. I visited the library and sat at a long table and removed several books from the full shelves, and I began reading. Suddenly I realized how quiet it was in the city and nothing was moving except for me. I realized there were no people or animals left. The whole city was empty and quiet. It was a city just for me and my needs. Where had they all gone?

♦　♦　♦　♦　♦

I woke up and, Misty was correct, I did feel better. Early morning was streaming through the bars of my window, creating a fence of shadows on the gray floor. I thought about how the forest had been sleeping, with Peter, Kat, and Theresa in its midst, with its birds, trees, ferns, rocks, rivers, grass, and now it was awake. I wondered whether Father had just tossed his covers aside, left his bed, what he was going to do on this particular day. Was he still working? Doing research? Did he have any new friends that were still alive? I thought about everyone else who awoke and began their days.

I felt strong and good. People were stirring in their various cells but the police hadn't arrived yet. Father had a purpose in life: creating me. Theresa had her purpose: Kat and God. What did the rest of us have?

The Story of Taste

I was an old woman made of body parts. They were aging as I was and I had retained them for a long time. I was maintaining my equilibri-

147

um. I lived in a city. My name was Dina. I was so ancient I couldn't count the years. I could hear a scraping sound inside my joints. I had forgotten longing. I couldn't feel much, smell, see, or hear well. I passed people I knew in the park, everything was hazy and dim.

"Dina, I'm catching the moon," an old woman called to me in the park. "Come and watch."

I hobbled closer. The moon spilled out of her hands and fell into mine. I turned that orange moon around and around in my wrinkled fingers. I kneaded its thick skin. But it wouldn't open up to me.

"The sky hurt me," I tried to explain to her.

"Close your eyes and open your mouth," she commanded me.

I snapped my lips shut.

"It's a surprise," she cajoled.

The air around me became pungent, sweet, sour, and citrusy. My old lips parted. Whatever she placed inside my mouth clung to me, like memories, although the body of it evaporated.

"That's what the moon tastes like."

I swallowed again and again to hold onto the dichotomous flavors. I had to ask her, "Then was it ever yours to give?"

I slipped my story into my notebook and hid it inside my clothes.

"I'm sorry, Misty," I yelled through the bars, "our deal is off. I can't take care of you."

"Shit," Misty said, "it's tough back in that park."

I easily bent the bars of my door. I could hear her better. I was glad to be back to my old self. I stepped through what was left of my door. No one was around yet. I punched the two hallway video monitors with my fists, shards of plastic fell and the electric wires dangled. I stopped to see Misty. She was still in her rags and reclining on her bed.

"Would you like to leave with me?"

"Naw," she said, "I don't mind it here." She grinned, her teeth browning like food cooked in oil. "But they ain't gonna get me in no shower this morning." She flapped her hand. "Besides, I've shown you all the good places I know about. You're good to go."

I heard shaking and whimpering from other cells, one where there were eight women all jammed together and another with six men wandering around. They stank of urine, feces, and anything else the body offered.

A woman with makeup and teased red hair yanked on her bars, "I want to get the hell out of here. Let me out."

"Okay," I said, bending the bars for whoever requested it. "Dispensation," I gave the woman with lipstick, mascara, and tiny clothes, whom I let out first.

"Whatever that is, I swear I didn't do it." She held up one hand and then gingerly stepped through the bars as though she might catch one of her high heels and trip. She stayed behind me while I opened several of the cells. "Hey, honey, a little makeup might help with your face. Shit," she said, "it looks like you've been put through a masher."

I was getting weary and my arms were beginning to ache after freeing seven cells. A few didn't want to leave. Some needed to do their time and others didn't want to leave, like Misty. There were about nineteen men and women in a phalanx behind me.

"Wow," the woman with makeup said, "you are amazing." She winked at me, "You should give me some of whatever it is you're on."

"I'm angry," I told her as she twirled her red sequin purse behind me.

"I know what you mean. I'm angry a lot too." She applied some more lipstick as she wobbled in her high heels. She pointed at a locked door. "That's the way out."

One policeman raised a club when I broke through the door. He was reaching for his gun. I knocked both weapons aside and held both his arms in one hand. Two other policemen tried to attack us but the crowd swarmed around them, pushing them down. I lifted all three policemen by their collars and threw them into an empty cell and locked it with their keys.

"You can't do this," one of them sputtered.

"We'll find you. All of you," another one threatened, grabbing the bars.

No one else had arrived yet. Then we all streamed out into the city and escaped.

Chapter Eleven

"Do you have some place to go?" the gasping woman in makeup asked me in an alley lined with garbage cans, old newspapers, empty bottles and cans. A car that had been stripped of its tires sat at the entrance. Everyone else had scattered. We fanned out and had finally stopped running. She pulled me into the alley. She was out of breath from running in her high heels. She scavenged through her purse and brought out several containers and a tube. "Here, let me do this." She opened a compact nestled in her palm. "Bend down," she ordered.

"Yes, I've been shown several places I can stay." I was thinking of the beach and the girl with her family. I wanted to see them again.

She cupped my face and applied powder, which puffed in the air, red on my lips, and she pressed blue and black onto my eyelids, even the one that was damaged. She refashioned an eyebrow. She concluded with blush on my cheeks. She assessed her handiwork, which was nothing compared to Father's. She lifted a tiny mirror toward my face but I only saw a little bit of me in the reflection.

"Not bad. My friend, Sparkles, he might be able to use someone like you and you could make some decent money. You can never tell what men want, you know what I mean." She looked me up and down. "Maybe a little S & M or even enforcement services for him." I didn't want to ask her what the initials meant.

She offered me a cigarette as she lit one for herself. I shook my head. "It's all illegal, of course." She winked at me. "Thanks for getting us all out. And without paying."

"No I don't want to meet Sparkles, but thank you." I tried to wink at her with my bad eye and eyelid, but they didn't work properly.

"Suit yourself. But if you change your mind and you need a job or money or something, you can find me around here." She left, walking languidly in her heels.

I had to decide where to go, so I sat behind the abandoned car and lay my head on the back fender. A smell from the garbage cans disturbed me, filled my nose with rot. I could hear an echo of footsteps approaching as if they were far away. They stopped, and I could hear ragged breathing nearby. The surface of everything in the alley turned white as if it had been burned when a man in black interrupted my thoughts by bending down, reaching for me. I leaped up, grabbed him by his high collar, lifting him.

I was about to reshuffle him with my fist when he said, "I am a flagellant Father, and I deserve this." His young, sculpted face turned to me as he pressed his hands together. His dark hair shone even though the light was dim. "This is rousing for worship. I'm levitating. God understands all my perpetual misunderstandings."

"God?" My mouth fell open. "Do you know Him?" I put him down in the dirty alley.

"Only in the most abysmal sense." He brushed off his dark clothes.

"I want to meet Him, God."

"I find Him in the space between dusk and light. But, my dear girl . . . you are a girl, aren't you? I can't really tell. Anyway, come with me to my church and we can try and find Him." He held out his hand, his brown eyes turned upward, toward me. "My name is Father Bill."

"Whose Father are you?" I inspected his clean black clothes by walking around him, looking.

"Yours, my dear, and I take it very seriously."

"Yes." I was mesmerized. I took his open hand. I could use a Father who knew God. One who wasn't filled with a monstrous love. "Who is your daughter?"

"I don't have one." He smiled. "I work with people like you. 'You shall hear the small and the large alike; you shall not be afraid of the face of any man; for the judgment is God's.' Deuteronomy 1:17." We began walking.

"Oh, my face!" I ran my hands over my individual features. Part of my right nostril had fallen off in my recent flight from jail. "I must look hideous to you."

"I'm not afraid of any face," he replied. "Men in my profession before me took care of lepers. I try and take care of all the people I meet in my neighborhood."

"That's kind of you." But he studied the sidewalks as we walked.

He looked up at me. "I, too, am being punished and ravaged by a disease within me."

"Maybe you weren't assembled correctly," I offered. "Or you need another Father to fix you." We angled past scrawny trees, handfuls of gnats, men in balled up bags and blankets sleeping in doorways with empty bottles lolling near them. "Could a doctor help you?"

"No." He shook his head, a strange smile on his lips. "It's deep within me. It doesn't show. My father did try and whip it out of me when I was a boy. It has also affected my faith." Tears brimmed at his eyes.

We stopped outside of a tall brick structure that was very different from Theresa's rustic church. The building was circled by a rush of stained windows filled with colorful renditions of wings, fish, men, women, night stars, flames, flowers, a sun and a moon. The windows grabbed a bit of sky and transformed it.

Sunlight became raw colors. The windows made me dizzy as if they were speaking to me. I pointed at one. "Are they trying to tell a story?"

"Aren't we all, in our own way?" He smiled a handsome smile as he unlocked the door.

When we entered the enormous room, it was dark, cool, and drafty with glints of gold on statues, books, cushions. I didn't need to bend or fold any of my limbs. Pews, worn by people's buttocks and palms into a smudgy soft brown wood, faced all that beauty. Light, filtered through all the church windows, made different dappled stories on the floor and pews with its bright red, blue, green, yellow, and blue. The colors flew around me as the light changed, whispering their tales, tattooing my body and Father Bill's. Even as we moved around the spacious room, they followed us, one story ending and another one beginning. It was roomy there, the opposite of the prison. I twirled on my incomplete feet, my arms outspread.

"I want my story to be on a window someday," I told him.

"Me too." He turned toward me as he scanned the interior. "What's your name, Child?"

"Mara. But I haven't been a Childcloud for quite a while." I pointed at a large wooden rectangular structure with open maroon curtains near the side wall. There was a chair inside of it. "What's that?"

"It's called a Confessional. It's where people can tell their stories, good and bad ones," he said. He smiled, "You confess to God for forgiveness."

I ran beside it, peeked inside. "Is He in there?" I inspected the box further. It was a tiny space with a chair and a lattice window covered with a curtain. "I don't see anyone inside."

"Did you want to confess some sins, Mara? You could confess them to me. I relay them to God and appropriate punishments are then meted out to you."

"I don't know," I answered shyly, my shoe, devoid of several toes, poked over the threshold. "Okay." I bent down, took up the whole space, plopped down on the chair.

Father Bill entered the box from another side. I could hear him settle in a chair. I could smell his sweet aftershave although my senses were dulling. Suddenly the curtain between us grew garrulous and fled to the side of the window so only the lattice separated us. Father Bill sat there, not looking in my direction. He was intent on the wall in front of him.

"Provocative," I gave him, having nothing else to give, except the money stuffed in my pants pocket.

"Pro," he said, "before or for in Greek and Latin. Vocare to call. Provocative, an adjective meaning to call forth or before, to excite or stimulate."

I clapped what was left of my hands together. "You are a father! You have dissected the word I gave you. Now maybe you will reassemble it differently. Take some pieces, leave the rest?" I chuckled with my grinding laugh.

He looked at me strangely. "Anyway, Mara, my child, tell me what troubles you. What has brought you here, to me, in this place, a holy place of God?"

"I have just come from jail where I understood, for the first time, my father's rage because everything he loved was taken away from him."

"I'm so sorry to hear about your family, Mara."

"He's trying, desperately, to bring them back. Is that wrong, Father Bill? Wouldn't you or I, if we had the chance, do the same thing? Wouldn't we do anything we could to get them back?"

"There are still many things I wouldn't do," he said, nodding behind the strange window.

"I wouldn't kill someone," I declared, "no matter how angry I was."

"That's good, Mara." His eyes searched the floor in his compartment, his private jail cell. "In God's eyes that's very good."

"Is it?" I wondered what I would do in Father's situation. Although I was made of human parts, why wasn't I human? Was I more than human? I would ask Father Bill sometime. Maybe he would have some answers. "Lately I'm not as sure what I am capable of."

"Yes, Mara, I know what you mean." He was pensive for a few moments then he snapped out of his own thoughts. "But there are basic rules established by God for our moral character and we must attempt to abide by them." His eyes darted toward the lattice. "Is there anything specific you want to tell me? Something you did to end up in jail?"

"That was a misunderstanding."

He nodded. "I understand. Did you want to tell me the story of your life? How you arrived at the alley where I found you?"

"I was born recently. I was a Childcloud too briefly, although my size hasn't changed much. My father was my world then. I wanted to taste the world outside of the small place I knew. I've met many people and animals, Gloves, Greg, Berserk the dog, Carl the driver, Theresa, Kat, Peter, Miss Elaina, Misty, Benjie the horrible, and many more people whose names I don't know. I've learned a lot and I'm still learning. I might fall apart before I've learned everything I want to know." At least now I had a story to tell. I couldn't tell him all of it out of fear he would run from me in horror.

"What's the matter with your body, if I can ask, Mara?"

"I don't know exactly why I'm coming apart. But Father might be able to fix me."

"Well, Mara, my child, He can fix many, many things. We'll have to see about you. Are you in pain?"

"Sometimes, but it goes away quickly. My body adapts."

"Pain can make you angry. Have you been to a hospital yet?"

"No." I shook my head.

"Well then," he said.

Outside, the hospital loomed over one whole block. Inside, the hospital was covered in blackness, according to my failing eyesight and color distortions. Although when the staff neared me, they were dressed in a transcendent white. Father Bill and I sat in a large room full of chairs that faced a desk, like at the church, except that it wasn't beautiful. A strong fluorescent light hovered over the desk from which people briskly approached and departed. A young woman was glued there, with telephones attached to her ears. In between talking on the phone, she told us to fill out forms and wait, along with the other people already waiting. I looked around, curious. A teenaged boy had an arrow through his shoulder and blood was pooling on the front of his Metallica tee shirt, an elderly woman was holding her dangling arm up with her other hand, a woman was crying as she rocked her swaddled baby, a man held his shirt to one ear, a family of three were huddled together in a corner weeping, a man in a leather jacket held a fist over one of his kidneys and small trickles of blood spurted over his fingers, staining them.

"Yes, Father Bill, you are right. This is where I belong. It looks like lots of these people will be trying to mend parts of their bodies today," I told him.

"Mara, we're in line to be seen, but this is a free city hospital, so it might be a while before a doctor can see you. I might have to go and do some other errands but I'll be back to see how things are going. Would that be alright with you?" He tilted his dark head away from me.

"Yes. Anyway, I know the way back to the church."

"Don't worry, Mara, please, just stay here when you're done and I'll come back and fetch you." Father Bill rose, brushing off his pants, and left, combing a hand through his dark hair. I must have fallen asleep or had a memory. It was getting hard to tell the difference. My head knocked against the hard plastic chair.

I was wearing pink satin pointe shoes and executing a pas de chat, then a glissade, ending with several fouette en tourant. Sergei was playing my prince. He held me in arabesque and turned me. My red gown with sequins flowed near my knees, grew salacious with the rhythm. I had waited too long to be a principal dancer. Sweat caught at my bodice and my tights, then gathered at my tiny tiara. I could see the faces of some of the other girls who couldn't dance as well. Sergei was near my left hip, and I was allowing the music to guide my body, swaying, jumping, the chaos of notes exciting my arms and legs. Nothing flailed; every inch of my body had its place according to the music and the choreographer.

Suddenly I landed with all my weight, my foot fracturing. The sound was of a lock opening and then all that pain flooded me. But the dance was beautiful and I wouldn't spoil it. Sergei glanced at me and knew. I finished the last part of Coppelia in excruciating agony. I wanted to scream, but I tried not to stiffen my gestures, to use the injured foot although I was making the broken bone worse. I collapsed backstage, behind the curtain.

I awoke with pain in my foot and someone calling my name, "Mara F . . . I can't read the last name. We're ready for you," the nurse in white was loudly announcing.

Someone led me down long corridors. Again I was sitting on a metal table in a room that was too small for me, and I was full of pain and longing. I had changed into a hospital gown and my clothes were in a pile at my feet. I didn't want to take what I needed from others in the way that both Father and Peter did to alleviate it. Some part of Father was inside of me, and I had understood it since jail. Father would have explained, "My darling Mara, we all live in a jail, even if it's our own body." The medical lights grew bright and came closer. A man, about Father's age, with blue eyes and a white jacket lifted my right arm and then let it fall.

He directed light over my face, my nose, my ear, my jaw. "Open your mouth please." I did. He was lost inside my mouth for a moment. "When did these necrotic episodes occur?"

"What?" But I understood him. I knew about medical terms from Father.

"When did you lose those parts of your mouth, nose, ear, and other areas?"

He stared into my eyes. "At different times."

"Did anything precipitate it?"

"It was spontaneous." I was matching his special medical words.

"I've never quite seen anything like this before. It's degeneration at a cellular level, as if you've been patched together and now the structure is coming apart." He frowned.

"Why now?"

"I don't know," he admitted. "Let me take some blood and tissue samples." It was a commandment.

"Okay."

He drew out a long needle, held my arm gently at the elbow, then plunged it underneath my skin. I didn't feel any pain, but his movements made me want to retract my arm.

"I'm going to call in some colleagues," he stated as he nodded to a nurse, who left the room.

He began scraping small bits of skin, fingernails, toenails, hair, moles, and bumps, a piece from my ear, nose, and lips. He wiped liquids from my nose, tongue, and ear for slides. I was afraid I might fall apart in his hands with all of his probing.

"I'd like to get some bone and organ samples and do a pap and gynecological exam. So we can figure out what's going on here," he told me as a phalanx of about ten men and women doctors entered the room. "But for that we need to put you to sleep." He administered a preoperative antiseptic to different areas on my body that turned my skin yellow.

I could hardly breathe in the room since the new doctors had fanned around the table, making the room tiny. The first doctor asked me to lie down on the table. I did. Someone wheeled over a table full of instruments I recognized, scalpel, retractor, needle holder, scissors, clamps, curette, probe, pliers. The mask was descending toward my face and then a frozen river inside me thinned, broke, and cracked into pieces that were drowning, floating, bobbing in the cold water under my skin. I sat upright and roared, all my muscles, skin, blood screeched. My nerves felt too close to my surface, like a fusillade, a constant firing. I was exploding. My body rebelled, could not endure another operation. The doctors shuddered and huddled away from me, some escaped out the door. I couldn't survive another operation even if, with their limited knowledge, they could help me.

"No," was all I managed to say before I grabbed two handfuls of their white clothes filled with their body parts and threw what I could against the walls of the room. A red light inside began blinking and screaming.

I grabbed my clothes and ran out into the corridor and then back to the large waiting room, everyone hurried away from me. Two policemen began to chase me as I ran through the room and exited onto the city streets. I hid behind the dumpster in a familiar alley. I closed my eyes, imagining my cells undividing, shrinking, until there was a miniature version left of me like one of those Russian dolls I had read about, one that was healthy, smaller. When I opened my eyes, the police had passed me by and were long gone.

I changed into my clothes and tucked the blue, tattered gown into a garbage can. I unearthed my notebook, wrote, *Longevity has its advantages as long you aren't being pursued. Don't allow life to take small bites out of you. I need a Father contraption for all the swift changes. I need some kind of god to guide me.*

The fireworks behind my eyes were increasing. My headache made widening circles around my head. I had damaged a wrist bone and a rib felt loose near my chest in my flight from the city hospital, a few blocks away. The hospital was perched over a busy street. I made my way stealthily back along the path I had memorized. I passed a crowd, silent over a hole in the pavement. I passed a man carrying a large stone. I passed a building whose doorway echoed every street sound and whose windows reflected everyone that wandered by. I walked by a park bench with a string of children drooling onto their shirts. I passed a woman, resembling the red-haired woman from jail, who bent over to talk to a man in a car, displaying her sexual components.

I called to her, but when the woman turned around, it wasn't the woman I knew. I missed all my familiar people and animals. Some days I needed someone to explain how the world worked.

"Where's God?" I demanded loudly in my gravelly voice as I burst through the locked church doors. I was being cheated again. Now the lock and chain were broken and dangling. They looked the same way I felt. "Father Bill?" I called tentatively, "I'm back. I want to meet God since He speaks to you."

But no one answered. It didn't seem right to be in the church alone, without parishioners or Father Bill, unless I was cleaning it. I ambled softly down the aisles toward the podium and cross. Colors from the stained glass windows brushed against my clothes, changing my pale shirt to red, then blue, then green. Stories dappled me as I moved by them.

Then I saw it. I hadn't detected it before because I had been losing my sense of smell along with my nose. The unsolved puzzle of a body lay strewn on the floor in front of the podium. At first I believed it was an animal sacrifice I hadn't learned about yet. Then I saw the decapitated head of a young woman, her eyes still open, resting on a pew. Her long brown tresses hung over the edge of the seat. An arm was left on a towel, a leg lay in a corner, another arm rested on another pew. I couldn't locate her torso. Using her good, young, fresh body parts raced through my mind for a second. But I didn't know what to do with them and couldn't find anyone who could put me back together again without an operation. After a few minutes, the body disgusted me. I bent down to examine an arm.

I heard footsteps and, searching the room, I saw Father Bill enter from a side door. He was wiping his hands on a towel identical to the one on the floor. His black jacket was open and his white shirt was splattered with blood.

"I thought I heard a noise," he said. "Mara, have you heard of transubstantiation?"

A big, beautiful word. I rose. "Yes, it's when bread and wine are changed during Mass into the body and blood of Christ." I wished Father would have enacted that transformation. "Although all we can still see are the bread and the wine."

"Yes," Father Bill answered, "I have sent this truly unhappy young woman to heaven to become an angel. We just can't see it. All we can see is the body." He smiled in a distant way as though he was sharing his thoughts with someone else far away. "I'm merely trying to ameliorate a mess that I made." He peered at the front door. "Did you break my lock?"

"I'm sorry. I was finished at the hospital."

"I told you I'd come for you." He gazed in my general direction but he didn't seem angry. "You should have waited for me. The hospital called here looking for you a little while ago. You made a fuss there, Mara. I'm surprised you actually came back here. They said that the samples they examined were abnormal, neither human nor animal." He looked directly at me. "What are you, Mara?"

"Why did you kill this girl?" I demanded. "It was a complete waste." I was yelling, mad at him. Father Bill didn't make any sense. Now we each knew one another's secrets.

"I told you there was something dark deep inside of me." He pointed to the eviscerated corpse. "I need to clean up now, Mara."

"I've seen dead bodies before. Have you done this often?"

"Why? Do we need to step into the Confessional?"

"You're a carcass of a man. There is nothing inside of you. You're foul and horrible, a monster." My agitated arms twirled in the air. My voice and my heart were shaking. I was going to explode again. "You had no right to kill her."

"Who is God among us?"

"Who wants that kind of god?" I mumbled, on the floor, trying to piece the puzzle of the woman back together.

"You're making a mess, Mara." He reached down, toward my arm.

"I contain women like her." I was babbling. I tossed his hand away. "I'm a terrible thing, not human, not animal."

"You don't know what you're saying." He patted my shoulder. "I'll fix it." He walked over to a closet door and reached inside of it.

"Consecratory necrophile," I spat at him. I could see the woman's bones through her skin. Her blood was obediently coagulating. Every part of her was open and exposed, unraveling precipitously.

"Unhappy abnormal," he replied calmly. He swiveled around with an axe raised in his arms. I noticed blood spots freckling the handle and blade. He ran a few feet towards me.

I stood, pulled his legs with my deformed hand and gripped his arm, which held the axe, with my other. He fell onto the floor on his back. The axe skittered away. I grabbed his axe and lifted it high over the black and white river of him. I didn't want to end him, but he left me no choice. If I didn't, he would kill me and continue killing. At least Father had a purpose in his destruction: It was creation. But didn't Father Bill believe that he was forming spiritual beings? Father Bill had to know that I would slay him rather than let him kill me. He had seen my strength, even though I was growing weaker. He had to know that he could die if he tried to hurt me and failed. I realized that dying was what he wanted. His eyes met mine and he nodded.

"I'm unhappy too," he whispered just as I brought the axe down gravitationally hard onto his heart, splitting it in two.

"Irrevocable."

Chapter Twelve

I was grieving and inconsolable. I had never wanted to slaughter anyone, any living creature, even someone who wanted to die. I had vowed not to kill anyone. Life experiences were so much more complicated than I had realized. I left both bodies there for the police to decide whatever they would. I washed up in a bathroom, cleaned my clothes, and walked out the church door, whose lock I had broken.

I wasn't sure where to go. The park? Jail? Under a bridge? Sparkles, where I could make some money? Somewhere no one would find me. And then I knew. Where there was a horizon of sky, water, earth. Everything was there. I took the subway. I wanted to get along with all the dead within me. We needed to reconcile. I was accumulating too many ghosts.

I was exhausted in the hurtling subway with its flickering lights. I leaned to the side and rested my head against the back of my seat.

My adolescent skin was black. I was wearing a dress with large embroidered flowers and some silver jewelry. I stopped in to see a girlfriend. When I entered I saw her mother gagged and bound to a chair. I knew the rebels were near but I didn't know that they had already arrived. Then I saw my girlfriend facing us, eyes closed. A man tore the clothes off her ebony body, her jewelry piled on the floor, his back toward us. Her mother's eyes darted to a knife lying across some partially cut vegetables on a table. No one else was in the room. I grabbed the knife and plunged it into his back. The man shouted and fell on the floor. My girlfriend collapsed near him. Another man rushed through the door, behind me. Before I could turn around, a machete pierced me, poking through the soft material at the stomach of my dress, eviscerating a big flower.

"Are you alright?" a man with soft brown eyes and blue jeans bent down and asked me.

"Yes." I wiped my eyes, could smell my stale, dirty odor, even with my misshapen nose.

"You were shrieking in your sleep."

"Nightmares." He didn't know the half of it.

"I can see that you've been through a lot. I hope you get better." The kind man left at the next stop.

I found a scarf decorated with coffee cups in the trash at my stop. It was a bit shredded, but I wrapped it around my lower face, so no one would notice how deformed I had become. I was losing bones, muscles, and organs more rapidly as time commenced. I was limping and dizzy. All of my senses were jumbled and fading. I hemorrhaged in strange, hidden places. My face no longer resembled the Daughter's face. Even the mole Father had placed had fallen off. I wasn't sure each day what part of my body would work.

I still felt terrible that I had killed Father Bill even though he didn't seem to know how to stop himself. I needed to be near the frothy waves, sun severed by clouds, sand brimming toward the rocks and crumbling wall, sand leaking into shoes and towels and drifting toward the water only to be pushed back again. Like anguish. How could Father live with himself?

I tried to remember "The Second Coming" by Yeats:

Turning and turning in the widening gyre
The falcon cannot hear the falconer;
Things fall apart; the centre cannot hold;

Mere anarchy is loosed upon the world,
The blood-dimmed tide is loosed, and everywhere
The ceremony of innocence is drowned;

The best lack all conviction, while the worst
Are full of passionate intensity.
I could only recall bits of the second stanza.
Surely some revelation is at hand;
A shape with lion body and the head of a man,
A gaze blank and pitiless as the sun,
. . . twenty centuries of stony sleep
Were vexed to nightmare by a rocking cradle,
And what rough beast, its hour come round at last,
Slouches towards Bethlehem to be born?

I hopped onto the familiar crumbling wall, sat down. Not as many people cavorted in the compromised sunshine of the beach. I scanned the families. I saw her. She was sitting on a blue blanket. She awkwardly stared at her arms and legs as though they weren't attached to her body. Her mother had an arm wrapped around her shoulder and was speaking. Her father patted her on the head and ran over to the ocean and dived in. I couldn't see the other children. The mother lifted the girl's chin toward her, said something, rose, and walked far down the shore. I watched the girl for a while. I found it soothing. I wondered whether Father Bill watched and eventually chose his victims or whether he knew them already. I briefly wondered about Father. The girl built small squares and circles with the sand, poured some water onto her handmade houses and buildings, then kicked them flat with her foot. She wrote something with a pencil in the sand. I couldn't read it from where I was sitting.

I leaped off the wall, sauntered casually down to the bathers and swimmers along the beach. Sand engulfed my shoes, making it difficult to walk. It was hot, but I liked the sound of the waves and the way they played hide and seek. I was hapless in overworn, numerous clothes, passing by people in bathing suits and shorts. I had a scarf wrapped around my face, while people wore an occasional hat, or thick, white sunscreen lotion. Many people recoiled. One of my fingernails fell onto a plastic picnic cooler. I ignored it and kept on walking. I stopped near the girl. Waves separated into white spasms. Corridors of sand stretched out around me.

"Hello," I said to her.

She didn't acknowledge my presence. It was as if I were already gone. She pulverized a sand castle, her hands sweeping it away.

"My name's Dina." I held out my damaged hand.

She still didn't look at me.

"Are you happy? Are you looking for someone?"

The girl looked up at me. Her dark hair and eyes wouldn't stay still. She looked right through me. She answered to someone behind me who wasn't there. "I have permission." Her voice was high and strangled. She wiped the sand again. Her face pulsed and collapsed. "Are you a friend?"

I smiled beneath my scarf. I sat, held out a hand. "I'm a friend." I faced the water.

The girl smiled, her features wriggling into furrows that changed constantly. I could read the word she'd engraved in the sand. It was *friend*.

Her toes shyly whisked sand back over the word. "Friend," she exclaimed loudly, pointing to her flat chest.

"What do friends do?" Time was still.

"Keep you company." Her hand slapped the top of her head. Her skin was translucent and I could see her veins and fat under the glare of the sunlight.

"Well then," I said, "we won't be alone together."

"Creatures are everywhere." Her arms fanned out.

"I have many inside me."

"Can they come out and play?" She cocked her head.

"They're hidden." I could feel the waves moving like muscles.

"Sometimes we eat them." She snapped her teeth, swallowed.

"Sometimes." I could see her mother posing by the ocean edge, stepping toward us. She would see me soon. I stood. "Goodbye, my friend. It was nice to meet you."

She was staring at the space where her sand houses had once been. I was already gone.

Curtains fell onto the faces of the people I passed on my way back to the subway. Or they jumped away from me. The subway ran next to a river and I exited near a stack of tall buildings. One was the library. I entered tentatively. I wondered if someone behind the desks would stop me. Ghouls were everywhere; a tattered man, worse than me, sat slumped, half reading in a corner chair, an elderly woman was pulling out strands of her stringy, white hair and stacking them in an oversized bag, and a man, whose odor even I noticed in my deteriorating condition, fondled books as he sauntered up and down the stacks. Suffering was everywhere.

I sat at a large wooden table, surrounded by shelves. A young woman at the end of the table whispered a poem to herself, a poem composed of colors, sounds, smells, touch. It began,

"In every accident there is the victim,

lingering like perfume after an encounter." She was weeping while cajoling everyone to write. She wrote the poem down, whether it was hers or not.

She turned toward me. "Are you wearing that scarf for religious reasons?"

I nodded. I moved to the shelf full of books about murderers. I fingered mysteries, spy thrillers, serial killers. None of those seemed right. I skimmed nonfiction about dysfunctional people who made mistakes and admitted them, people who believed they were vampires or werewolves. I tried Science, research on the body and diseases. I fell into a chair with *Cloning: How to Live Forever*. I wanted to assuage the terrible feelings writhing inside of me. I closed my eyes, told myself: you are capable of doing anything if you did that.

Gold Chinese letters filled the blue sign across from me. Red and black dragons perched around the ad for BETTER LIVING WITH HONG'S NOODLES. I straddled the balcony fence at the top of the tallest office building in town. It wasn't that high, so I could see an old man with a bent back and cane, sticks in a bundle on his shoulders, crossing a street. And a woman, younger than me, teetering on an old bicycle, laundry neatly folded over the back wheel. I smelled smoke from the factories, hot oil and spices used in woks at lunchtime. I imagined my skin slipping away, into negative space. I thought of my ancestors and mother and father's faces when they saw me. I wanted to apologize to everyone, even to the window left open. But I have nothing since my husband left. No children. I am not strong. I swayed with my toes barely touching the railing. I held my hands over my ears as I jumped, so I didn't have to hear my body break as it hit the ground.

My eyes flipped open. I didn't think I could do that either. Suicide.

"Regurgitate," I remarked as I raced to the library bathroom and made it in time to a cool, white porcelain sink. I rinsed my mouth with water from the faucet. I didn't have many teeth left.

Back in the large library room, I decided that I was safer with a dictionary, which would increase my vocabulary, so that I would have more words to give. But my failing eyes drifted to the word "kill," which was "to slaughter for food" and "to deprive of life." "Murder" implied "premeditation and therefore with full moral responsibility." Was there less responsibility when the action wasn't planned?

I slipped deeply into the cushioned library chair, the thick, heavy book resting against my lap. I felt at home in the library. I was tired. I was going blind like Kat, but my other senses were dimming too. My bones creaked. My skin and clothes smelled of decay. I couldn't even imagine how I looked, a shredded scarf around my face and head, my hair falling out, one eyebrow missing, not many fingers left. And those were the parts of me that were visible. I began to close my eyes.

If I died here what would they do with my body? Would they locate Father? What would they do to him? I opened my eyes again quickly.

I left the library, took the subway to the bus station, where buses hissed to their stops, reinventing their destinations. My remaining $98.46 was more than enough for the one-way ticket. People hurried by briskly. Conversations, sneezing, brakes, humming engines, bus doors opening and closing stained the background of my poor hearing. I was about to sit and wait for my bus when I saw Misty in the corner, strumming the ribs of her grocery cart. I approached her, but she didn't recognize me, married as I was to my fetid body, and she flattened herself against the wall, moved away from me.

"Unblessed," she shrieked at me, afraid.

"Misty, it's me, Refrigerator."

Her mouth sewed itself shut again. She stared at me. "Yes," she said, "Refrigerator, a good name." Her windmill arms quieted. "There are more rooms to show you, full of the unsavory, if you dare."

"You need to take your medications," I told her gently.

"I have another weed to pull." Her eyes flung themselves toward me. "What happened to you?"

"I'm ill. Don't worry, it's not contagious."

"I'm already part gravel." She dug through her cart, pushing aside a packet of light bulbs, crumpled, beige sheets, a man's shoe with the laces hanging. "Look what I found!" She held up a crutch and cackled. "Good for crowd control. Here." She thrust it toward me.

"Thank you. I could use it."

"Are you lost again?"

"I'm leaving now." I would miss them, Carl and his dog, Berserk, Misty, Theresa, Kat, Peter, the girl on the beach.

She tilted her head. "Anything received must be shared."

"Here," I held out the rest of my money, cascading the bills and coins into her palms. She scooped them quickly inside her tattered sweater.

Misty's face lit up. "You have to turn the sign off when you're gone."

"It's hard living in the city. I can see that. It's a fractured life." I was already leaning on the crutch.

"That jail was full of glued appendages. You were smart to recover from it." She winked at me.

I could see dirt collecting in the fold of her eyelid, the supratarsal crease. My appearance wasn't much better. "Goodbye."

"My hair's made of glass. I can't find a dress unless I unzip myself."

I patted her hand. She was agitated.

"We can't go anywhere near them." She nodded at all the people.

"Are we really that different from them?"

"We're not welcome here. But we can scavenge for photographs of the party." She unearthed a picture of a cow, showed it to me. "Nothing's happened here before."

I turned away from her. "Please take your medications." Otherwise there wasn't much left to tell her. My bus had arrived and my body still obliged my mind's wishes. I teetered up the bus steps using the crutch. The driver assisted me. It was the hour when daughters considered killing their fathers, sons their mothers. I sat toward the back. The seat hurt my buttocks and my stomach seized at the effort. I rested. I wasn't sure whether I had failed in my life experiences or not.

I picked an aisle seat because my impending blindness would occlude me from seeing much of the scenery as it flew by out the window. I could hear a dog's frenzied bark echoing from the station. I had to shoo a pesky fly away continuously with my hand. I removed the notebook Miss Elaina gave me. I could write even though I had sustained a hole in my arm and attendant bruises. As the bus began moving I squinted at the streaks on the window.

I would relinquish my past while the white line behind the bus unspooled. We passed the river, whose water no one could drink or swim in. Was there any part of me not ready to break?

The bus was empty. My spine was disassembling; rents in my flesh began to fester, one part of my neck unbuckled. My nearby window passed a smattering of clouds, trees thrashing in a wind, a slanting house. The weight and gravity of that wind would be too much for me now. I had no choice but to embrace what I had become, a life amid death, my patchwork body failing me.

"Moribund," I gave myself, no sound, only my lips moving. Then I fell asleep.

I was arranging letters into words I didn't know. Maybe it was another language. Maybe it was a language I already knew. I was young, large, a Childcloud, fresh, lovely. My mole was perfect. I separated the letters, brought them back again, rearranging them. Some of the words were familiar. I opened a book and marveled at all the sentences. They were meaty with good, complex words. Someday I would understand them.

I enjoyed the smells in the house, a human, food. Every object gave off some kind of odor, a lemony table, a minty rug, a footstool like tea. The sounds were still overwhelming, the tick of a clock, scraping of a chair, liquids pouring, opening and closing drawers, doors, lids, books. I tasted everything, licking the fireplace, the toilet, lamps, locked windows. Especially the windows, which I imagined held the flavors of clouds suspended in air. I was curious. What were they for? Why wasn't I allowed out there?

My father started to open the door into my room, "My darling. . . .

I awoke to a young boy, in shorts with cropped red hair, pulling on my sleeve. My elbow became disjointed, my scarf fell with the tussling, revealing a bit of my face.

"Yuck," he grew closer to me, "what's wrong with you? You look scary. You were crying really loud in your sleep. You look

really gross." He ran back to his mother, who wore a gold head-
band. He climbed into her lap.

She whispered, "Be nice to people who are different, Donnie.
You can do that for me, can't you?"

The boy nodded.

An older lady with blue hair a few rows in front of me turned
around and mouthed hello to me. "Are you okay?"

I nodded. "Yes, I'm fine."

The bus rumbled and sometimes passed a car too quickly, but I
grew used to the rhythm. I was in pain, my kidney and heart ached,
but I extricated my notebook, the one that had belonged to Sandy Shane. I pulled out and crumpled the two pages I had already
written on. I held it close to me so I could see what I had written.

Three Ways of Looking

1. *The living wear the arms of the dead,*
   I fall into them, out of context.
   I make the same mistakes without trying.
   My mind wonders what will happen next.
   I'm expecting a monster.

2. *Every evening the moon comments*
   on what I should have done.
   Memory is reasonable, explaining
   what there was to escape from.
   The monster was what was left behind.

3. *Stretch skin. Rearrange eyes. Wiggle*
   ears. Protect the brain. Arms are easily
   removed. A monster on a country road.
   A monster rising from a dark city alley.
   A monster in the sky. Look. Look away.

173

Part IV

Mara F.

Chapter Thirteen

The bus didn't stop too far from our house. It took me a long time to hobble there. I held in my entrails as best I could. Leaning on the crutch pushed my weaker organs around so I had to press my viscera back into place. Father opened the door a crack when I knocked, using my two remaining knuckles. Father stared, evaluating what he could see of me. I was plagued by flies since leaving the bus. They clustered around my body, landing on parts I couldn't reach. He threw the door open, shooed the flies away.

"My Mara, my darling daughter, you're in terrible shape. Come in, come in. You know that the various anatomical parts of you degenerate differently, depending on the age, lifestyle, and genetics of the person you received them from as well as the date the part was attached." He looked into my fading eyes, "How do you feel, sweetheart?"

I dragged myself and my crutch inside the house, noticing that nothing had dramatically changed. "Lackadaisical."

He roared with laughter as I sat on the sofa. "Thank you for the word," he said. "You haven't changed much. Except, well, let's see under all that wrapping. You're like some kind of a present under all that material." He leaned my crutch against the maroon sofa. "Would you like something to eat or drink? Are you hungry, sweetheart?"

I shook my head. "How are you, Father? I've thought of you often." He was unwinding the scarf, which caused me some pain.

"I am predictable." He looked at me clinically. Not horrified like the other people but not compassionately like Theresa, or even Misty in her own way. "I'm back doing research. I go on. What about you, Mara? You must tell me what you have been doing and why you were compelled to leave." His eyebrows crawled toward his forehead, and his glasses, the same, familiar eyeglasses, slipped further down his nose, his bone-colored hair kicked out in every direction. "You know that you could never fail me. I never thought you would. I wondered what had happened to you, even with the note."

"I did something horrible."

"What?" His eyebrows twined together.

"I killed someone."

Father roared with laughter again. "People die every day for no good reason."

"I was in the country and then the city."

"Oh," Father said. "Did you tell anyone about me and you, about us or our research?"

"No."

He smiled. "Good girl. Which place did you like better?"

I handed him my notebook. "This explains everything."

"I will treasure this." He placed the notebook on a table and touched my nose, jaw, ears, cheeks.

I winced. "I'm falling apart."

"We all are, darling daughter, some of us faster and some slower." He lifted one of my arms, let it drop. "Hmm, the deltoid flap is compromised. Are you in much pain?"

I nodded.

"Some of the older parts are separating from the newer ones. But the tissue and skin are degenerating too. I could do more tests and determine how widespread it is. Whether it has reached the bones, the organs, or the brain."

But we both already knew. I heard soft footsteps in the kitchen. "Is this what happened to the other Maras?"

Father nodded, his head shaking all those strands of white hair into fragments. "But it happened much more slowly since I was there to replace the exhausted or nonfunctioning areas."

"Why do I remember or imagine so many of their deaths?"

"Probably because that was the most recent emotionally evocative moment in their lives and it permeates every cell. So memory can be retained in the parts too."

"Are there any others out there like me, like the Maras?"

Father shook his head. "None that I know of."

I didn't want to consider the alternative ways he obtained body parts. I'd had enough. The soft footsteps grew closer.

"Gloves, get out of here. We're busy. Go," Father exclaimed to a black and white cat with an indentation where a collar had been.

I didn't have the energy to ask about the cat. I sighed. My legs were swollen. I had terrible indigestion although I had hardly eaten anything in the last few days. Every piece of me that Father had assembled hurt. I looked at the cat. It was starting all over again. "Come here, Gloves."

The cat looked at me with its yellow eyes as if asking a question. Then, without any hesitation, it jumped into my pathetic lap. It was wonderful, soft fur and the rhythmic purring, although its weight bothered my legs. She didn't care how I looked. I was growing thinner than air.

"I don't have the strength I used to have." I thought briefly about breaking her neck to save her from pain, like the previous Gloves, but I was too weak.

Father said, "I'll carry you down to the lab." He shooed the cat away.

My bones shifted uncomfortably in his arms as he easily lifted me.

"Imponderable," he gave me.

He placed me on the dreaded operating table, brushing my sad clumps of hair out of my face. He shined a pinpoint of light from a tiny flashlight into my poor eyes and moved it around. "Try and follow the light with your eyes." The Photographs consoled me, Mother and Daughter, even the Scientist. At least now I understood their meaning, the context of their surroundings, their lives. He strapped me down.

"Use me." It was what I wanted. It was my fate.

"My little apomixis," my father murmured in one of my ears.

"Yes, Father," I whispered, knowing I wasn't born from fertilization but created from body parts.

"I thought you were the one," he shook his head, his wild hair flying. "My Mara, I love you. I have always loved you and I always will."

"I love you too, Father."

Then he moved to a corner of the room and spoke into a tiny microphone attached to a recording device. "Mara Five has returned. I'll remove her brain for use in Mara Six. It seems to be the one resilient transplanted organ that has survived. My special adhesive compound has its advantages and disadvantages. I'm very, very close. . . ."

I thought I could hear someone moaning and kicking furniture in a room in the house although the anesthesia mask was approaching my ravaged face. A girl. I couldn't tell if it was upstairs or inside of me. Was it a Mara or someone else? I had finally created my own memories.

I remembered Father, with tangled dark hair, his eyeglasses slipping, kissing my fat baby arms, tickling my stomach and underarms; a mobile with shiny, colored shapes dangled just out of my reach; I was crawling toward the maroon sofa; my first bicycle ride, Father and Mother's dark heads trailing; my first day at school; Mother's lovely back at the kitchen making breakfast; my bedroom window broken by a baseball; Father wiping tears from my eyes with a handkerchief; Father teaching me letters, then words, then sentences. I was reading. We began to toss words back and forth, describing one another and everything around us, including the fascinating and beautiful world.

"Transgression" was the first word I gave him.

The Author

Laurie Blauner is the author of three previous novels, *Infinite Kindness*, *Somebody*, and *The Bohemians*, all from Black Heron Press, as well as seven books of poetry. A novella called *Instructions for Living* was published in 2011 from Main Street Rag. Her most recent book of poetry, *It Looks Worse than I Am,* was published in 2014 as the first Open Reading Period selection from What Books Press. A poetry chapbook was published in 2013 from dancing girl press. She has received a National Endowment of the Arts Fellowship as well as Seattle Arts Commission, King County Arts Commission, 4Culture, and Artist Trust grants and awards. She was a resident at Centrum in Washington state and was in the Jack Straw Writers Program in 2007. Her work has appeared in *The New Republic, The Nation*, *The Georgia Review, American Poetry Review, Mississippi Review, Field, Caketrain, Denver Quarterly, The Colorado Review, The Collagist,* and many other magazines. She lives in Seattle, Washington. Her web site is www.laurieblauner.com.

CPSIA information can be obtained
at www.ICGtesting.com
Printed in the USA
LVOW01s0003170916

504939LV00008B/10/P